YOU ARE SPIDER-MAN...

It looks like you might be able to sneak the hostages out without the Shocker noticing—he's so busy ranting and raving. There's an emergency exit only a few steps from where they're being held. But there are too many for you to carry them all, so first you have to untie them. Silently, you creep down the wall.

The hostages see you. Their faces are filled with anguish and fear, but luckily they have the sense not to cry out and warn the Shocker. The ropes that hold them are no problem. You reach out to snap the nearest cord . . . just as your spider-sense goes off like crazy.

You freeze, your feet on the wall, and your hand on the rope. What is your spider-sense warning you about? Maybe the Shocker is about to attack. Should you keep trying to free the hostages, or go after the Shocker now?

For Zoey and Lani
R.C.

YOU ARE SPIDER-MAN

Richie Chevat

Illustrations by Neil Vokes and
Michael Avon Oeming

BYRON PREISS MULTIMEDIA COMPANY, INC.
NEW YORK

AN ARCHWAY PAPERBACK
Published by POCKET BOOKS
New York London Toronto Sydney Tokyo Singapore

AN ARCHWAY PAPERBACK *Original*

An Archway Paperback published by
POCKET BOOKS, a division of Simon & Schuster Inc.
1230 Avenue of the Americas, New York, NY 10020

Copyright © 1996 Marvel Characters, Inc.
A Byron Preiss Multimedia Company, Inc. Book

All rights reserved, including the right to reproduce
this book or portions thereof in any form whatsoever.
For information address Pocket Books, 1230 Avenue
of the Americas, New York, NY 10020

Byron Preiss Multimedia Company, Inc.
24 West 25th Street
New York, New York 10010

The Byron Preiss Multimedia Worldwide Web Site Address is:
http://www.byronpreiss.com

ISBN 0-671-00319-4

First Archway Paperback printing August 1996

10 9 8 7 6 5 4 3 2 1

AN ARCHWAY PAPERBACK and colophon are
registered trademarks of Simon & Schuster Inc.

Edited by Howard Zimmerman
Cover art by Mike Zeck and Phil Zimelman
Cover design by Claude Goodwin
Interior design by MM Design 2000, Inc.

Printed in the U.S.A.

"Watch out! It's gonna blow!"

A shriek of terror shatters the air in midtown Manhattan.

"It's a bomb!" shouts a policeman, as he struggles to help a fallen woman to her feet. "Those nuts are going to blow up Trump Tower! Everyone take cover!"

High above the madness in the street an amplified voice rings out.

"We give the city of New York thirty minutes to agree to our demands! If not, the destruction of this symbol of decadent waste will be just the start of our revenge."

Alone in a doorway, you watch the scene of mass hysteria without moving. To all appearances, you're just Peter Parker, ordinary citizen. But, in your other identity, as Spider-Man you could ... you ponder that for a moment, What *could* I do?

Suddenly, a different voice cries out.

"Cut!"

As if by magic, the panic melts away.

"Okay, people," says the voice on the loud-speaker. "That was good. Take a break while we set up for the next shot."

The movie extras sigh in relief and move as a group to the table where coffee and doughnuts are laid out for them. Of course, that's what they are—extras, actors in a movie that's being shot on location in New York City. It's *Fatal Action III*, a movie that you have a special interest in because one of the roles is being played by your wife, Mary Jane Watson-Parker.

"What do you think, Tiger?" Mary Jane says, walking toward you in her costume as police detective Emma Steel.

"I think those nasty terrorists are in trouble," you reply with a grin.

"Hey, Mary Jane! You have to get ready for the skyscraper stunt!"

It's one of the production assistants. He points up to a nearby skyscraper where the movie crew is getting ready.

"C'mon," MJ says, leading you by the hand. "Walk me up there."

You follow her into the building, and ride up in the elevator. Together, you walk out onto a large balcony many stories above the street.

"There she is," says a tall young man.

"Who's this?" he says to Mary Jane. He steps forward and looks at you with a grin. "Another pesky fan?"

You know it's only a movie, but that's your Mary Jane who's walking out to the edge of a twenty-story drop.

"Actually, he's my biggest fan," Mary Jane answers. "This is my husband, Peter. Peter, this is Chip Alvarez, the director."

"Hi," you say, shaking hands. "I've seen all of your movies."

Suddenly you realize that your spider-sense is acting up. Something is wrong here, there's some danger nearby, but you don't know what it is.

"Nice meeting you," says Alvarez. "But we're on a tight schedule here. If you want, you can watch from over there."

He turns to MJ. "Mary Jane, we're all set up. Are you ready?"

"Sure," she replies. Then she gives you a wink. "Don't get into trouble, Tiger, I might have to rescue you."

She follows Alvarez to the edge of the balcony. Now your heart starts beating for real. You know it's only a movie, but that's your Mary Jane who's walking out to the edge of a twenty story drop. And you don't even have your web-shooters ready in case something goes wrong. Is this what your spider-sense is warning you about? Is the stunt too dangerous?

GO TO PAGE 76.

My spider-sense never lies, you think, twisting in midair *away* from the stuntwoman.

You close your eyes as you swing around. When you open them, the stuntwoman is gone! Instead, you see the glass and steel wall of the Trump Tower.

If I hadn't stopped, I would have hit that wall like a ton of bricks! you say to yourself.

Something is playing tricks on your senses, creating illusions. Now the stuntwoman seems to be on your right, when a moment ago she was on your left.

"Help her!" someone from the movie crew yells. "Why don't you help her?"

As hard as it is, you ignore the screams and try to think. The stuntwoman may not be where she seems. She may not even be in danger. You have to solve the problem of the illusion. But you know one thing—an illusion usually means Mysterio!

You also know there's one thing that Mysterio can't fool—your spider-sense. Closing your eyes, you concentrate. Suddenly, you can sense it—it's coming from above you, from the roof of the Trump Tower. In a flash you have swung your way up there and come face to face with the master of illusion, Mysterio.

"A little slow today, are we, Spider-Man?" he says to taunt you.

"Sorry," you snap back. "I stopped on the way to catch a flick. Seen any good movies lately?"

"Movies? You dare speak to me of movies!" Mysterio's voice seems to echo off the surrounding buildings. He waves his fist at you. "It's because of you, Spider-Man, that my career in the movies is over. I was the greatest special-effects master of all time! Those fools working today are children compared to me."

"Yeah, well, I think it's time you got back in the playpen," you say. Then, dodging sideways, you shoot a web-strand at Mysterio, trying to trap him. But for once he *is* too fast for you. With a puff of smoke he seems to vanish.

My spider-sense tells me he's still nearby, you think. But that stuntwoman is still in danger. I'd better make sure she's okay before I go after Misty.

You flip off the edge of the building and into free fall, breaking your descent a hundred feet below. There—you see the stuntwoman! And you're sure she's really in danger.

"Hold on, ma'am," you say in your best super hero voice. It's only a matter of seconds before you've spun a web under and around her, making sure she can't fall. A few seconds later and you've pulled her to safety.

"Spider-Man, am I glad *you* showed up," says Chip Alvarez when you return the stuntwoman to the balcony where the whole crew has watched your rescue of her.

"Yes, we're *all* glad to see you," says Mary Jane with a big smile.

"Thanks," you say. "Just your friendly neighborhood Spider-Man. But I have to be going." But even though everything seems all right, you notice your spider-sense hasn't stopped tingling. Does that mean Mysterio is still lurking around? You decide to go look for him.

With a wave of your hand, you launch yourself into the air, and do some fast web-slinging back to the Trump Tower. But it's too late. All traces of Mysterio have vanished.

GO TO PAGE 31.

I don't think that stuntwoman was ever in danger, you think, racing across the rooftop. I'm going to put Mysterio where he can watch *lots* of movies—in prison!

At the edge of the rooftop, you jump out into space almost a thousand feet above the earth. Closing your eyes again, you let your spider-sense guide you toward Mysterio. Somehow, he's gotten behind you, on a lower terrace of the Trump Tower. You swing down easily, planning to fall on him from above.

"Gotcha!" you cry, feeling triumphant as your web snakes around Mysterio, holding him fast.

"You may think you have me, Spider-Man," he replies, calmly. "But look who else you have."

Suddenly the scene changes. Instead of Mysterio at the end of your web, you're holding the cable that the stuntwoman is hanging from. Instead of reeling in a bad guy, you're swinging an innocent person above a terrible drop.

"No!" you shout. Closing your eyes, you realize it's just an illusion. You do have Mysterio trapped, but he's making it look like you're attacking the stuntwoman.

"This won't work, Misty," you say, pulling him closer with your web.

"Oh, won't it?" Mysterio replies. There's a sharp snapping sound, which makes you sick in the pit of your stomach. Opening your eyes, you see that the real stuntwoman's cable has snapped and Mysterio has made it look like you did it.

Your spider-sense tells you *this* is no illusion. Horrified, you release your web-line and leap down to save the stuntwoman. You're seconds too late as she hurtles toward the skyscraper. But at the last moment, the movie crew manages to get a net under her.

"Mysterio!" you scream in anger. But the bad guy has used this moment of confusion to vanish.

Quickly, you swing over to the movie crew. They are gathering around the stuntwoman. You already hear the sirens of the ambulance in the street below.

"She's hurt, but she'll be all right," says Chip Alvarez. "No thanks to Spider-Man!" he rages. "I'm calling the police. You're going to be arrested on charges of assault and attempted murder!"

"No!" you protest, backing away. Your spider-sense is still tingling and you can't figure out why. You're confused, and you're not the only one. You can see the eyes of the entire cast and crew are on you. The looks on their faces are filled with anger and fear, except for one. Marry Jane looks at you in hopeless confusion.

That woman almost died and it was because of me, you think over and over as you swing away. I let a jerk like Mysterio get the best of me, you think. I should have known where my first job was—to make sure that woman was all right. I'm not fit to be a super hero.

Disheartened and confused, you go home. That's it, you say. I'm through being Spider-Man.

END

"Gotcha!" you cry, feeling triumphant as your web snakes around Mysterio, holding him fast.

I don't have time for sneaking around, you say to yourself after a few seconds' thought. That Shocker is just crazy enough to start knocking off hostages. You leap across the street and up to a street lamp, where you hang upside-down.

"Hey Shocker!" you yell at the bank windows. "It's me—your old pal Spidey! Wanna come out and play?"

Seconds tick by. Nothing happens.

"What's the matter, Shockey baby?" you shout. "Mama won't let you out to play with the big boys?"

Silence again. You begin to sweat. Maybe the Shocker can't hear you. Maybe he's changed and doesn't care about dumb challenges. Maybe. . . .

SKRAAST!!

Without warning, a mighty blast of high-pressure air crashes across the street like cannon fire. It snaps the lamppost you were hanging from like a matchstick and rips a ten-foot trench in the pavement.

16

Good thing my spider-sense warned me, you think, from the wall of the bank building itself. Or I'd be picking asphalt out of my pants right now.

Seconds later a figure in a brown and yellow costume strides down the steps of the bank. The Shocker moves to the edge of the hole in the pavement and looks down.

"At last!" he crows. "I've done it! I've killed Spider-Man! Finally, after all these years, I have my revenge!"

"Yoo-hoo, Shockey, up here!" you call. "As the man said, the reports of my death have been greatly exaggerated."

As the Shocker turns, surprised and furious, you send twin web-strands shooting at him, but he dodges them at the last moment.

You see the Shocker raise his arms—a signal he's about to send another vibro-blast your way. You easily leap to the street, somersault forward and come up within punching distance just as he sends a shock blast to the wall you just left.

Your fist cracks into the Shocker's jaw, sending him crashing to the pavement.

"Sleep tight, Shockey," you say, raising your web-shooter and preparing to wrap him tightly in a net of webbing.

"The bank!" someone in the crowd shouts at just that moment. "It's collapsing!"

You turn your head to look. Sure enough, the wall of the bank is starting to crack where the Shocker's last blast hit it. Your spider-sense screams, giving you a split-second warning that the Shocker is sending another blast at you. You roll out of the way just in time. As you come up standing a few yards away, you kick yourself mentally for getting distracted. You almost had the Shocker tied up, now he's on his feet again. But you ignore him and swing toward the bank to see if you can web that wall up so it won't collapse.

Maybe I should lead him away from this crowd. But how do I do that?

You leap out of the way as another vibro-blast is let loose. You feel the rush of the air as it flies by harmlessly.

On second thought, maybe I'd better put him away right now.

IF YOU TRY TO LEAD THE SHOCKER
AWAY, GO TO PAGE 143.

IF YOU DECIDE TO KEEP FIGHTING HIM
HERE, GO TO PAGE 78.

18

"You know there's nothing I'd rather do than party with you, MJ," you say regretfully. "But I can't goof off until I know what those bad bozos are up to."

Soon you're flying high above Times Square. So far, no sign of any bad guys. You take a breather and glance idly down at the Jumbotron television display.

The first thing you see is a televised interview with that nut Mason, the politician who's been attacking you.

You're about to swing away when something in Mason's look catches your eye. What is it? Fear? Insanity? Maybe you should go down to that TV studio and start investigating *him* a little.

IF YOU GO TO THE STUDIO,
GO TO PAGE 107.

IF YOU MOVE ON,
GO TO PAGE 81.

"The hostages are still my first priority," you say to yourself. "Whatever my spider-sense is warning me about, I'll just have to face it when it comes."

With that thought you reach out and snap the rope holding the nearest hostages.

BAROOM!

With a tremendous roar, the ceiling above the hostages explodes.

Booby trap! you realize. That's what my spider-sense was warning me about!

You have only a split second to save the hostages from death. You raise your web-shooters and send twin jets of webbing overhead, trying to create a net to catch the falling debris. It seems to work. A ton of brick, steel and concrete rain down, but none of it falls on the hostages.

"I did it!" you say, and at the same moment, you feel something like an iron girder strike you in the side. The rush of air tells you it was a blast from the Shocker. It drives you into the wall, stunned and breathless. As you lay there, the Shocker appears over you.

"Bye-bye, Spider-Man," he says. "We had other plans for you but this is even better than what we'd hoped for."

He aims his vibro-blasters at the ceiling above you and, with a blast, another shower of debris comes falling toward you. The last thing you remember is a jagged boulder of plaster and concrete coming down at you.

When you wake up, you're on a stretcher being loaded into an ambulance.

"Don't move, Spider-Man," says the medical technician. "You've been hurt pretty bad."

From the pain shooting through your body, you can tell that he's right. You're lucky just to be alive. It will take weeks to recover from this, maybe longer. By then the Shocker will be long gone. You'll never find out what he meant by his *plans*. And who did he mean by *we*? You'll never find out now.

END

I can't trust the Hobgoblin, you think, turning in mid-swing. I'd better make absolutely certain everyone is safe.

It takes two swings for you to land on the roof of the museum just a few feet from the bus. As you do, you hear the Hobgoblin gloating in the street below.

"He runs! See how he runs!" The villain cackles madly. "Today I have shown the world what a craven coward Spider-Man is! Soon he will be a dead coward!"

From the museum's roof you see the Hobgoblin flying off over Central Park on his jet-glider.

"Well, I guess that's one that got away," you say to yourself as you yank open the door of the bus.

"Thank you, Spider-Man," MJ says, giving you a secret smile. "I know my husband will really appreciate this."

Satisfied that everyone is okay, you're about to swing away when you see Alvarez climbing onto the museum roof. Your spider-sense starts buzzing at the same time.

"You coward!" he screams at the top of his lungs. "How could you just let that maniac get away? How could you do that? You let him waltz out of here and now he's free to come back any time. That's it, people. We're closing down production, until we can be sure we're safe!"

Alvarez turns and stalks off before you can get in another word. The whole time you're on the lookout for Hobgoblin's return, but soon your spider-sense stops tingling.

The remaining actors look at you, not knowing what to say. All except Mary Jane.

"Don't take it too hard, Spider-Man," she says. "He's just upset."

Somehow, that doesn't make you feel much better.

GO TO PAGE 24.

"Well, that worked out well," you say sarcastically as you and Mary Jane walk downtown.

"Don't take it so hard, Tiger," she says, gripping your arm. "You did the right thing and you know it."

"Yeah," you grumble. "But how come the right thing feels so wrong?"

There's a loud noise coming from around the corner. It's a political rally for your favorite mayoral candidate, Bob Mason.

A small crowd has gathered, and as you draw near you hear what they're shouting.

"Spider-Man must go! Spider-Man must go!" You stand there for a moment, your stomach churning with anger.

"You heard them," you say and manage to laugh. "Spider-Man must go . . . so let's go."

You've turned around, but suddenly your spider-sense sounds an alarm. A sudden shriek from the crowd makes you turn back. A winged figure has swooped over the candidate's platform. In a flash you recognize the green costume and the outstretched wings. It's the Vulture!

"Help!" Mason screams into the microphone. "It's another one of those super creeps! He's going to kill me!"

The Vulture grabs the mike from Mason.

"Not so tough now, are you, Mason?" he cackles. Even at this distance you can see the wild gleam in the Vulture's soulless eyes. He lashes out with his fists and starts tearing apart the podium. But so far he hasn't made any moves to hurt Mason. The crowd, which scattered at first, is edging back toward the stage.

"Get out of here!" they're shouting. "Leave him alone!"

"I'd better do something," you say to Mary Jane.

"For that creep?" she replies. "Let the police handle it. There are some officers here already. Besides, if Spider-Man shows up, it might make the crowd do something stupid."

GO TO PAGE 130.

"This is too easy," you say to yourself, swinging *over* the tunnel entrance rather than into it. "There's got to be something fishy going on."

You land noiselessly in the deserted park on the other side. And there in front of you is the other end of the tunnel. Carefully, you sneak up to the edge. Your spider-sense is tingling, telling you made the right decision—the tunnel is a trap.

The Hobgoblin has someone with him. You creep inside, hoping to surprise them. But just as you cross the entrance to the tunnel, the cloaked figure tilts his jet-glider into a banked turn and roars straight at you. You easily dodge out of the way, somersaulting and coming out of your roll ready for action.

Springing up, you launch yourself into a web-swing at the villain.

You're about to connect with your feet, when your spider-sense tells you that bad guy number two is coming up behind you. You twist out of the way and the Vulture flies past, colliding with the furious Hobgoblin.

"That's what I like to see—team work!" you laugh, closing in and hoping to catch them off balance. You connect with a side kick to the Vulture, keeping him on the ground, but the Hobgoblin comes up with a flaming pumpkin bomb. You duck down, but it gives the Hobgoblin a chance to remount his glider.

"I don't need a team to destroy you," the Vulture rages.

From above, the Hobgoblin sends two of his bombs hurtling down at you. You leap sideways and use the highway overpass to haul yourself higher. Now there's a lull in the fight. Both the Vulture and the Hobgoblin have flown up higher, just out of your reach. With no tall structures nearby, you can't get to them and they manage to avoid your web-lines.

Just then the Hobgoblin's glider soars close enough for you to snag it with some webbing. A lucky break, you think as you rush aloft on your line. Or did he *let* me snag him?

"Okay, Hobgoblin!" you shout. "Now we're going to have some fun!"

You're about to swing around to the top of the sled, when the Hobgoblin turns. It's as if he was just waiting for you to get close. Out of his hand darts a needle-sharp razor-bat, cutting your web-line. You instantly begin to fall and though you try to shoot out another strand of webbing to catch the glider, you just miss it.

"You're lucky this time," the Hobgoblin yells in his eerie voice as he and the Vulture fly out over the river. "We have other plans. But the next time we meet it will be your doom!"

"I don't understand it," you say to MJ that night when you're back home in your apartment. "It's not like those creeps to fly away without even trying. Why do I keep thinking they were up to something?"

"Maybe because they were," MJ says and points to the television set.

There on the screen is a replay of your run-in with the Vulture and Hobgoblin. But somehow it's been changed. Someone has doctored it to make it look like you're horsing around with them instead of fighting them.

"They set me up!" you exclaim. "Now I'm *really* mad!"

GO TO PAGE 80.

"What the hey!" you say, trying to sound cheerful. "You're right, MJ, let's party hearty."

"That's what I like to hear," she says with a big grin.

An hour later, the two of you are in your best duds. Stepping out of an elevator in Rockefeller Center, you're about to enter the legendary nightclub, the Rainbow Room.

"Hey, these movie people really know how to throw a party," you shout to MJ as you enter the ballroom. A band is playing earsplitting rock music and the dance floor is jammed with couples moving to the beat.

"Mary Jane! Having a good time?" It's Chip Alvarez, the film's director. He plunges into a discussion with MJ, talking over their upcoming scenes and the character she's playing in the movie. You can't really hear what they're saying over the noise, but at that exact moment your spider-sense starts tingling.

You decide to find a place to change into

your spider-gear because you're sure trouble is coming. You motion to MJ that you're going to the bar and slowly make your way through the crowd. Your spider-sense is buzzing. Suddenly, you feel a strong hand grip your elbow.

"Hey there, you're Mary Jane's husband, aren't you?" It's Al Markham, the special-effects director.

"Yeah, hi," you say weakly. Your spider-sense is still sounding, but you can't shake off the dizzy feeling you have. It's almost like someone has drugged you. But how?

"Say, you don't look so good," Markham says. "How about some fresh air?"

"I don't know," you mumble. You don't want to leave MJ, not when there may be danger nearby. On the other hand, you need to change into your Spider-Man costume. What should you do?

"You look like you're about to faint," he says. "Come out here on the balcony and have a seat."

IF YOU STAY IN THE BALLROOM,
GO TO PAGE 104.

IF YOU GO ON THE BALCONY,
GO TO PAGE 120.

That same night, you and Mary Jane are relaxing at home.

"Let's watch a little TV," you suggest.

"Sure, Tiger," she says with a yawn.

The TV screen lights up with the late news. A large, red-faced man is looking out at you from the screen. The news caption under his face reads: "Bob Mason, Mayoral Candidate."

"This city is in trouble!" Mason is saying. His supporters cheer wildly. "Lawlessness is running rampant. Costumed super crooks break the law in broad daylight. And the so-called super heroes stand by or even help them. Just today someone calling himself the Shocker robbed a bank in midtown and made off with three million dollars. I for one can't see much difference between a costumed creep like the Shocker and the one who calls himself Spider-Man. They're both menaces to our society!"

The next morning, you're on your way to

work at the *Daily Bugle* and MJ is heading back for another day of filming on *Fatal Action III*.

"Share a cab, Tiger?" she asks as she steps toward the curb. You decide to go with MJ— the *Bugle* can wait.

So the two of you hop in a cab and head over to the Museum of Natural History, where the day's shooting has already started.

"Wow, it looks like a war zone," you comment as the cab lets you off on Central Park West. Tanks, armored personnel carriers, jeeps and other pieces of military equipment are parked up and down the street. And in the center of it all sits an ordinary-looking city bus.

"There you are!" A young production assistant comes running up to MJ. "They've moved up your scene—better get into costume!"

Director Chip Alvarez hurries by, surrounded by three assistants and Al Markham, the special-effects coordinator. He waves and gives you a big smile. Suddenly, your spider-sense goes off.

"Today you're going to see how tough your wife can be," Markham says as he follows after Alvarez. "Wait till you see how we blow up that bus!"

"I, I can't wait," you stammer. Your good mood has evaporated. Your spider-sense warned you yesterday about the accident with the stuntwoman. What is it warning you about now?

You watch with growing fear as everything is made ready for the next scene. In this shot, the movie terrorists have taken a busload of passengers hostage. Mary Jane's character, a police detective, has managed to get onto the bus and is in a face-off with the terrorist ring leader. It's MJ's big scene.

The camera is in position, and the actor playing the head bad guy stands on the steps of the bus. Naturally, he's dressed all in black and has a make-up scar across his face.

I wish all bad guys were so easy to spot, you think.

MJ takes a step forward and glowers at the movie bad guy.

"I'll tell you something, Lorenzo, this bus requires exact change and *I don't think you have a token!*"

"Oh yeah, cop lady?" the actor spits back. "Well I brought along my little *bus pass*." He holds up a shiny black automatic weapon. "Now how about a free transfer?"

"It's creeps like you who give public transportation a bad name," MJ says with a wild gleam in her eye.

Hey, she's good! you think. I'd have surrendered five minutes ago.

Suddenly the smile vanishes from your face. That itchy feeling down your spine means just one thing—your spider-sense is tingling stronger than before. Something is about to happen, but what?

"Too bad you can't afford cab fare, *copper*!" the terrorist is sneering.

"Too bad is right," roars another, ghostlike voice that seems to rise up out of the sewers below your feet. An eerie cackle follows it and, without having to see, you know who that voice belongs to: the Hobgoblin.

A split-second later the crazed villain flies into view on his jet-glider. His weird death's-head mask grins under his orange cowl. In his hand he holds a pumpkin bomb.

"Run!" someone screams. As if someone has pulled a switch, the street instantly turns into a scene of mass hysteria.

Time for my own costume change, you think as you hot-foot it toward the nearest trailer. Before you can say "friendly neighborhood Spider-Man," you've changed into your Spidey clothes and burst back into the street. But what a difference a few seconds makes.

Most of the street is now deserted. But there, in the middle of Central Park West, thirty feet above the ground, hovers the bus that was being used in the scene. All the actors who were playing hostages in the movie are still on board, along with the movie terrorists . . . and one more person. Cold fingers of fear seize your heart as you realize that red-headed figure on the bus is the love of your life, Mary Jane.

You stand in the shadow of the trailer, trying to size up the situation before you make a move. As you do, the Hobgoblin's spooky voice, like a metal file being dragged over gravel, rings out. He points a bone-like finger at Chip Alvarez, who is cowering behind one of the tanks parked in the street.

"You there!" the Hobgoblin commands. "Unless your movie's producers hand over ten million dollars in cash in thirty minutes, this busload of actors will be reduced to a busload of cinders."

"Ten million?" Alvarez sputters. "Thirty minutes? How . . ?"

With an easy bound, you leap the thirty feet to the top of the tank.

"Never fear!" you shout, trying to sound glib and cocky. "Spider-Man is here!"

GO TO PAGE 141.

"**A**lways listen to your spider-sense," you tell yourself for the umpteenth time and you jump out of the way. In that instant, the illusion vanishes. There's no train, as you knew. Instead, you see Mysterio fly past, riding one of the Hobgoblin's spare gliders. A second later and you would have been crushed by it.

"You jumped!" Mysterio wails in the darkness behind you.

"Sure. I knew it wasn't a subway train, but of course I knew that you knew I knew, so you figured I *wouldn't* get out of the way."

For once, none of the Sinister Six have anything to say. You use the moment of silence to slip under Doc Ock's guard, roll forward and come up ready to deliver a knockout blow. But at that moment, one of the Hobgoblin's bombs goes off. It doesn't strike you but the shock wave loosens a rain of bricks and concrete from the ceiling, which has been greatly weakened by the Shocker's blasts. The last thing you see as the roof of the tunnel caves in is Doc Ock's gloating face.

The next thing you know, you're floating upward through a haze, your vision cloudy, your body one giant ache. Slowly, you remember where you are and begin to push away the fallen timbers and debris.

"Whoa!" you groan as you sit up on the tunnel floor. "That was some party."

You glance around. There's no sign of the Sinister Six. But under the dim light of a bare bulb you see a small tape recorder with a hand-written note attached. You stumble over, and read the note. It says "Play Me."

You press the Play button, but you have a feeling you know what you're about to hear— the gravely voice of Doc Ock.

"We could have finished you, Spider-Man," the recording says. "But watching you squirm and suffer will be much more fun. Never fear—we'll meet again. And when we do, it will mean your doom."

Feeling worn out and frustrated, you stumble out of the tunnel and head home over the dark, deserted streets of the city.

GO TO PAGE 136.

I can't remember exactly how that special-effects equipment works, you think.

Doc Ock holds MJ overhead with two of his steel arms. As he does, you concentrate everything into a desperate headlong leap, trying to somersault forward and knock the control box out of Ock's human hands. For a split second you think it just might work, then you feel Ock's two free claws come clamping down on you, pinning you mercilessly to the ice.

"Nice try, Spider-Man," he gloats. "You did exactly what I predicted you'd do. Now I predict something else: You're finished!"

For once, Doc Ock might be right.

I really blew it this time, you think. Big time.

END

For a split-second you think it just might work, then you feel Ock's two free claws come clamping down on you . . .

I just missed squashing myself like a bug on a windshield, you think. Someone is making me see things that aren't there, and my guess is that someone is Mysterio.

Mysterio is a master of illusion who uses his hypnotic skills and special effects technology to make people see what isn't there.

"Spider-Man, do something!" It's Chip Alvarez again, shouting at you to help the stuntwoman.

It seems like an eternity, but it's really only a second or two until you're rushing toward the glass and steel wall of the Trump Tower.

There! you think. He's up there. You can feel your spider-sense, alerting you to the real danger—not the stuntwoman, but your enemy, Mysterio. He's up above, near the top of the Trump Tower. You quickly begin to climb.

"He's climbing away from her!" someone yells. "He's going to let her fall."

You know that to them it looks like you're

40

ignoring the stuntwoman's plight, but you have no choice. This is the only way you can save her—if she truly needs saving. You shoot a web-strand up toward the roof and swing yourself up, landing just yards away from a strange caped figure whose head is enclosed in a clouded glass bubble—Mysterio.

With a flick of your hand you shoot a web-strand at his helmet, trying to trap him. But Mysterio is too fast. In a puff of smoke he disappears and then rematerializes at the other end of the roof.

Moments later you've vaulted through the air and sent a web-net arcing through space in an attempt to snag Mysterio. But again he vanishes. This time he reappears on a rooftop three buildings away.

He's using his hallucinogenic gas, you realize. That's the only way he could trick me like that.

Now that you know what he's up to, you feel confident you can capture him. But there's still the stuntwoman down below.

IF YOU GO AFTER MYSTERIO,
GO TO PAGE 12.

IF YOU RETURN FOR THE
STUNTWOMAN, GO TO PAGE 114.

You just can't stand by and ignore her calls, even if it means taking some risks.

You shoot your web-lines, kick off from the building and swing toward the stunt-woman. At least, you swing toward where you *think* she is. Your spider-sense is screaming like a hundred fire alarms, but it's too late. You crash into an office and send shards of glass falling to the street below. In agonizing pain, you gaze around in disbelief. Through the broken window, you can see the movie crew rescuing the stuntwoman—no thanks to you.

It's a slow, agonizing journey home over rooftops, and you barely making it back to your apartment before you collapse, bleeding and hurt.

For now, this adventure is over.

END

"**H**old it!" you say to yourself. Got to listen to my spider-sense. It's never wrong. The danger must be right here with the hostages.

A quick glance at the ropes binding the hostages shows you what your spider-sense was reacting to. The hostages are booby trapped. Cutting their ropes or moving them will set off a blast in the ceiling, collapsing a ton of debris on them.

"What's wrong, Spider-Man," says an evil voice behind you. "Having trouble with the knot?"

You look up and you see that the Shocker is now on a staircase and is looking straight down at you.

"Let me give you a hand," he says. He presses a button on the wrist of his costume and the rope you're holding snaps apart. At the same instant, a vibro-blast goes off in the ceiling. A ton of concrete, brick and steel are about to rain down on the hostages. But thanks to your spider-sense, you've already begun spinning a safety web to hold the pieces of the ceiling in place.

"Well, I'd like to stay and chat," the Shocker gloats. "But I see you've got you're hands full." And with that, he ducks out the bank window. By the time you get all the hostages to safety and get outside again, the Shocker is long gone.

Well, you think, at least I saved the hostages.

"The money! Spider-Man, you let him get away with the money—three million dollars!" It's Mulroney, the police captain. He looks at you accusingly.

"I didn't let him . . ." you begin. Just then a television news crew runs across the street and shoves a microphone in your face.

"Is it true, Spider-Man?" the reporter begins, her face only inches from yours. "Is it true you allowed the Shocker to walk off with three million dollars?"

Feeling disgusted with the whole thing, you flip backward onto the top of a police van and from there you swing yourself onto a nearby rooftop. I've had enough for one day, you think. Besides, I'm late for work.

GO TO PAGE 31.

You've already begun spinning a safety web to protect the hostages and hold the pieces of ceiling in place.

It doesn't take you long to make up your mind.

I don't know why, you think, but I have a feeling that wherever MJ and Peter Parker go, the Sinister Six is bound to show up sooner or later. You finish cooking breakfast, and in a little while you and MJ are heading downtown for the site of that day's filming—Madison Square Garden.

You get off the bus and walk into the arena, and MJ explains what's supposed to be filmed this day.

"In this scene, the movie terrorists take control of Madison Square Garden during a hockey game," she explains. "They hold both teams and all the fans for ransom. Until I show up," she adds with a laugh.

You walk out into the vast open space of the arena. On the ice below, real hockey players and stuntmen are practicing their moves, pretending to be two opposing teams. The film crew moves about, still setting up lights and equipment. Thick cables snake along the seats and stairs. Several hundred extras fill the seats closest to the ice. One of Alvarez's assistants is having them practice cheering and booing.

You see the special-effects wizard Al Markham huddled with Alvarez, the director, in a couple of seats near the rink.

As MJ goes to change, you figure it's time for you to change, also. Slipping away, you find a place to change into your Spider-Man costume. Then it's an easy climb up into the girders where you have a great view of everything going on below. You see Alvarez and Markham still talking. As you do, your spider-sense starts tingling.

I guess I was right, you think, something's going to happen here. You watch as Markham and his assistants set up a scene in which it looks like one of the hockey players gets shot. As you wait, you're beginning to wonder if you made a mistake. But your spider-sense is still buzzing. Down below, they're finally getting ready to start filming.

"Okay everybody, take your places," the assistant director announces through a megaphone. "And let's make it look real."

As if on cue, a thunderous crash echoes across the giant arena and a cloud of smoke issues from one of the entrances. Your heart leaps as out of the cloud rides the Hobgoblin on his jet-glider, followed by the Vulture, the

Shocker and Doctor Octopus—four of the Sinister Six.

"All of you, stay where you are!" Doctor Octopus commands, his voice a roar. He waves his snakelike steel arms in all directions. In spite of his warning, his appearance sets off a panic. Actors, hockey players and extras all rush for the nearest exit. In the middle of all the confusion, it's hard for you to pick out Mary Jane. You think you see her, crouching behind some of the movie equipment.

Just stay there, MJ, you think as you begin to climb down. Spider-Man is about to go into action. But there are only four of those creeps. Where are the other two? What are they up to?

You decide to stay out of sight until you figure out what the Sinister Six want. But that soon becomes clear, as Doc Ock seizes a microphone and begins talking.

"There is no use in rushing for an exit," he declares, sounding as if the whole thing is one big joke. "You will find they are all blocked. Try to open one and a bomb will go off. But there's no reason to panic—yet. I'm sure the mayor of this great city will meet our demands for your release—a measly twenty million dollars. And if he doesn't, then I'm equally sure your end will be quite painful, thanks to the radiation bomb we have hidden in the basement."

Could this be a hoax? you wonder, clinging to one of the support pillars. Or is there really a bomb? Doc Ock wouldn't set it off while he's in the building, but maybe he's rigged it to go off by remote control. My first step is to find that bomb and disarm it, then get a door open so these people can get out.

Hiding in the shadows, you slip to the floor behind some seats and duck into a corridor. The problem is, that bomb could be anywhere, you think. Where should I look first?

As you try to decide, you see two familiar figures hurrying along the hallway. It's Alvarez and Markham. You swing ahead and drop to the floor in front of them. As you do, your spider-sense, which has been tingling all along, starts buzzing like an alarm bell.

"Spider-Man!" Alvarez cries. "Don't hurt us."

"You've got it all wrong, fellas," you say. "I'm one of the good guys. I'm trying to find that bomb and disarm it."

"You are?" Markham says. He doesn't sound like he believes you. "But the news reports said . . ."

"Look, I can't explain it all now. But I need you to help me find that bomb and disarm it."

Markham looks at Alvarez, who nods. "Okay, we'll trust you. The fact is, we've already found the bomb. We were going to call the police, but we can lead you to it, if you want."

"What are we waiting for?" you ask.

Markham and Alvarez set off at a run, heading down some stairs and along a bare hallway.

You know you're on the same level as the ice now, but you're not sure exactly where. Then you find yourself standing in front of a door.

"It's in there," Markham says. "If you're really not working with those criminals, you'll go in and disarm it."

"No problem!" you say, and reach for the doorknob. As you do, something makes you stop. Something has been nagging you for a couple of days now. It seems that your spider-sense hasn't been working right—or has it? It's been going off when there doesn't seem to be any danger around. Is my spider-sense warning me about the bomb on the other side of the door? Or is there something else going on here?

IF YOU GO THROUGH THE DOOR,
GO TO PAGE 97.

IF YOU DON'T GO THROUGH THE
DOOR, GO TO PAGE 68.

It's almost pitch black inside as you feel your way along the ceiling of the abandoned subway tunnel. Then your spider-sense comes alive like a clanging alarm clock. There's danger—big danger—up ahead.

The tunnel curves downward and, near the bottom, you see lights and a clump of shadowy figures. Cautiously, you creep a little closer. Then you see something long, metallic and snakelike dart through the air.

Doc Ock! you almost cry aloud.

I should have known, you think, mentally kicking yourself. All these villains showing up at the same time—it's no coincidence. Doc Ock has gathered together his old team—the Sinister Six!

As you edge even closer, you remember all the times you've faced Doctor Octopus in the past. A brilliant scientist, he was caught in a terrible accident during one of his experiments. Not only did it drive him mad, but it fused those four snake-like arms to his body and, as you know too well, each arm ends in a jaw-like steel pincer.

You wonder what these villains have in store for you now. At least you notice one thing about them hasn't changed: as usual, the Sinister Six are not getting along very well.

"What are we waiting for?" the Shocker is complaining in his loud, harsh voice. "I say we finish him off now."

"As usual, your mind has all the cunning of a sledgehammer," says the Chameleon. "What is the glory in defeating Spider-Man by merely blowing him up?"

"Who cares about glory?" the Shocker replies. "I want to see him suffer."

"Suffer?" the Hobgoblin interrupts in his other-worldly voice. "Who has suffered more than I?"

"We've all suffered at his hands," adds the Vulture. "That's why we want his end to be painful and humiliating."

"Yeah?" shouts the Shocker. "But what if he gets away again?"

"Enough!" Doc Ock commands. His four steel tentacles shoot out in all directions. "Your squabbling only proves why *I* am the leader and you are the followers. We have *all* suffered at the hands of that cursed spider-monkey. That is why he must pay in full. We must take away everything that is important to him, just as he has denied us our lives. And what is most important to someone like

Spider-Man? His reputation as a miserable do-gooder."

As you listen, Doc Ock goes on to outline his plan for your destruction, a plan that the Sinister Six has already started to put into motion.

"We must take away the one thing he craves—the affection and high regard of the public, that mass of cowardly sheep who cower behind the protection of self-styled crusaders like Spider-Man. We must make Spider-Man hated and feared the way we are hated and feared. Then we can watch him suffer before we finally destroy him."

"I just want to watch him being destroyed by my vibro-blasters," the Shocker grumbles, but Ock silences him with a look.

"My plan is already working," the crazed mastermind gloats. "And thanks to that politician, Bob Mason, there's even a growing movement against our little hero."

You realize that now is the perfect opportunity to catch the Sinister Six off guard. On the other hand, there *are* six of them. Maybe you should sneak away and get some help, like the Fantastic Four if they're in town.

IF YOU ATTACK THE SINISTER SIX NOW,
GO TO PAGE 116.

IF YOU DECIDE TO GET SOME BACK UP,
GO TO PAGE 124.

I t only takes you a second to decide.

I can't risk attacking him now, you think. I've got to see if I can get the Vulture to let Mason go. *Then* I'll clobber him!

As Mason shrieks in fright, the Vulture tosses him into the air, where he hangs for a split second. Then he begins the sickening drop to the pavement below. But you've been waiting for the Vulture to pull a stunt like this, and in no time at all you've spun a webbed safety net to break Mason's fall. He drops into it and you lower him to the street.

As soon as you get Mason down to the street, the throng of people runs forward, screaming at you. Some of them are even throwing things—bottles, cans and rocks. Even more confusing is the fact that your spider-sense is tingling again.

"Let him go! You're killing him!" they scream at you.

"Killing him?" You're so startled you forget to shield yourself and an empty soda can

54

hits you on the head. What is going on? Someone or something is making these people think you're *attacking* Mason instead of saving him. It must be Mysterio, that master of illusions—*that's* what your spider-sense is picking up, you think. He's using his tricks to hide himself, but he must be nearby. You look to a nearby rooftop and there he is—with the Vulture, high overhead.

Mason, who by now has struggled free of the webbing, stands up and starts screaming.

"You saw it!" he yells, his face red with anger. "They were working together! The Vulture and Spider-Man! Help me, all of you!"

"No!" you shout. "It was Mysterio! Look, up there!"

Mysterio waves scornfully and the Vulture laughs madly, then wheels off, carrying Mysterio with him. But the crowd must still be blinded by Mysterio's hallucinogenic gas. With a heavy heart, you go off to find MJ.

GO TO PAGE 80.

Still shocked by what you have just seen, you decide to take MJ home before doing anything else. You rush into the hallway and find her in the stairwell, still heading downstairs with the other frightened guests.

"Peter, what happened?" she asks, clutching you with relief.

"I'll tell you on the way home," you say. "Let's get out of here."

GO TO PAGE 136.

They won't strike now, you realize. They'll wait for Peter to contact Spider-Man.

In a flash, you've ducked out of the deserted ballroom and climbed out a window. Keeping a safe distance behind, you follow them across the city. You're just in time to see the glider and its two passengers disappear into the darkness.

The East Side subway tunnel is over there, you realize. The one that's been abandoned. Carefully, you follow them inside.

GO TO PAGE 51.

I can't take a chance that someone might get trampled, you think, turning in mid-air and heading for the stands. Besides, MJ might be in that crowd.

Mysterio is standing with his back toward you, concentrating on projecting his illusion. He doesn't sense you until you've swung right into him, knocking him down. Instantly his illusion vanishes. The crowd turns and sees you tying up yet another one of the Sinister Six. They cheer insanely as you hoist Mysterio on a web-line and leave him dangling over the penalty box.

"That's for unnecessary roughness," you say as you swing away.

Two left, you think. The Chameleon must have beat it, so that leaves Doc Ock.

"Come on Ock," you say, standing in the center of the ice. "You're a lot of things, but you're not stupid. How about giving up and saving us a lot of hard work?"

"Never!" Octopus roars back. He lumbers

toward you from across the ice and you notice he's having trouble keeping his footing. Suddenly, you have an idea. You grab a hockey stick.

"Okay," you say almost gleefully. "If you want to play, let's play!"

You reach into the nearby equipment box, grab a handful of hockey pucks and drop them on the ice.

"Childish games will not help you!" Ock shouts, running awkwardly closer. His arms will soon be in range.

"Aw, come on, Ock," you say. "You wouldn't kick a man who was down on his puck, would you?" And you seize the stick and send a puck shooting across the ice with a powerful slap shot. It hurtles toward the mad scientist, but you don't stop to watch. As fast as you can you shoot the rest of the pucks at him, some on the ice, some flying up into the air, more than a dozen shooting for Doc Ock at the same time.

"Stop!" he shouts, twisting to avoid the missiles. Exactly as you hoped, he begins to slip and slide, losing his footing.

"No!" he screams. He drives two of his arms into the ice to keep himself from falling. But that's also what you expected. You make one more shot, driving a puck at head height, right for Doc Ock's face, then another right after it. The two remaining arms snake out and catch them.

"Hah!" Doc Ock laughs, holding the pucks aloft.

"Good save," you say, swinging overhead. "But don't you notice something funny about those last two pucks?"

Ock looks at the pucks he caught in his claws.

"No!" he screams. For they're not pucks at all, but bundles of webbing that have now gummed up his claws. Ock tries to shake the webbing loose, but you swing over and drop on him from above, knocking him unconscious.

"Well, Ock," you say as you bind him securely. "I hate to say it but it looks like I put you on ice."

Wild cheers from the crowd fill the arena. For the first time in a long while, you really feel like a hero. The actors and movie crew come rushing toward you. The first one to reach you is MJ.

"Spider-Man!" she cries. "You saved us!"

You'd like to take her in your arms and give her a big hug but you don't. Your spidersense is screaming. Lifting your right hand you shoot a web-line across MJ, catching her in a web lasso.

"Help!" she cries. "Spider-Man is attacking me!"

"Give it up, Chameleon," you say. MJ, or what looks like MJ, struggles for a moment, but then the real Mary Jane steps out of the crowd. The Mary Jane who is tied up in your

60

webbing suddenly shape-shifts into his true form—the Chameleon.

"Nice going, Spider-Man," says the real Mary Jane as the crowd cheers again. "But how did you know it wasn't me?"

You could say that you knew the Chameleon was still on the loose. You could say that your spider-sense warned you. You could even say that, hey, a Spider-Man ought to know his own wife when he sees her, right? But you don't say any of those things. You just laugh and shrug.

Finally, you say, "Hey, I know a real star when I see one."

THE END

I can't stop now, you think, and swing toward Doc Ock. You dodge over one of his metallic arms and under another, shooting a line of webbing over his eyes to momentarily blind him. You're about to swing in to deliver a knockout blow, when a scream from the stands makes your head whip around. Out of the corner of your eye, you see it's Mary Jane and she's about to be crushed by the panicking crowd. A second later, a sharp pain in your side tells you you've let down your guard. Doc Ock has recovered and one of his claws struck you just before you could move away. You manage to swing away, but you're hurt.

You swing toward the panicking crowd, which is running away from the illusion Mysterio has created. Dropping down swiftly, you get a line around MJ and haul her to safety. Without a word you drop down again. As you do, the illusion vanishes.

Mysterio must be leaving, you realize as

you swing toward an exit where the crush of people is the greatest. Finally, the panic dies down.

You rush back to the ice, but you already know what you're going to find there. Doc Ock, Mysterio and the Chameleon are gone.

You haul the Hobgoblin, the Shocker and the Vulture into center ice and wait for the police, who arrive a minute later.

"Spider-Man!" the first policeman to arrive shouts in fear. "We heard you joined the Sinister Six!"

"It's not true!" one of the actors protests, rushing up. "He saved us!"

Soon the whole crowd is joining in, including MJ who comes running up.

"It's true, he fought them off," she says. "He's a hero!"

"Hey, Spider-Man," yells one of the film crew. "You're the real star of this movie now! I think we got some of that battle on film. Want to see it?"

"Uh, no thanks," you say, laughing. "And do me a favor—don't plan a sequel!"

THE END

I can't risk getting those hostages hurt, you think. As much as I hate the Shocker, rescuing them is my number one job here.

You turn to the police captain. "Try to distract the Shocker," you say. "Keep him talking. I'm going to try to get in and get the hostages out."

"Okay, Spider-Man," the captain says.

"Shocker!" he shouts through the megaphone. "This is Captain Mulroney. Don't do anything rash. Let's talk about this!"

The Shocker's voice is gruff. "No talking, cop. And you tell Spider-Man if he comes one step closer the hostages' lives will be his responsibility."

"I'm sending Spider-Man away," Captain Mulroney replies. "Just don't hurt anyone."

That's your cue to get going. You climb up the side of a building and, when you're sure you're out of sight of the bank, you swing out over the roof and drop down on the rear wall of the bank building. You can still hear the police captain talking to the Shocker.

Keep talking, Shockey, you think. Tell them how much you hate me. That'll take a couple of hours, at least.

A minute later you're creeping along the bank's high ceiling on the main floor. You rest on one of the chandeliers and look around. There they are. The Shocker is by one of the windows, which he has blasted open. The hostages are huddled in a corner, tied together. The lights are off and it's easy for you to blend in with the shadows.

"Spider-Man!" The Shocker is yelling now. "Give me Spider-Man and I'll release the hostages!"

I'll give you Spider-Man, you think. But not the way you mean. Silently, you creep down the wall.

The hostages see you, but luckily they have the sense not to cry out and warn the Shocker. The ropes that hold them will be no problem. You reach out to snap the nearest cord just as your spider-sense goes off like crazy.

You freeze. Maybe the Shocker is about to attack. Should you keep trying to free the hostages, or go after the Shocker now?

IF YOU TRY TO FREE THE HOSTAGES
FIRST, GO TO PAGE 20.

IF YOU TAKE ON THE SHOCKER,
GO TO PAGE 43.

The Vulture is too unpredictable. There's no telling what he'll do if you try to trick him into letting Mason go. You know your only real option is to force him to let the politician loose and just hope you can keep him from getting hurt.

With a sudden twist, you swing toward the Vulture, let go of your web-line and fly through the air toward him, feet first. Catching the villain off guard, your boots strike him with the impact of a battering ram right in his ribs.

"Ooof!" You hear the air being forced out of the Vulture's lungs and at the same time, you see him lose his grip on Mason.

"Help!" the politician screams.

"I've got you," you say as you grab him with one arm. With the other you shoot a line of webbing toward the opposite building. Keeping your eyes open for the Vulture, you swing with Mason toward the nearest rooftop.

"Let go of me!" Mason shouts, right in your ear.

66

"Uh, you can't be serious," you say. Mason looks down, his eyes bulging with fright as you speed through the air, and then he clamps his mouth tightly shut.

The Vulture, who was stunned for a moment, fell out of control, but now he has glided back up into the air.

"Keep the little rat," he yells at you scornfully. "I've got better things to do than waste my time here!" And he flaps away, disappearing over the buildings.

You drop to the tar paper of the building's roof with a light thud and deposit Mason on his feet. You actually feel sorry for the guy, who is white-faced and shaking with fear.

"Hey, you're okay now," you say. But he only glares at you and runs for the stairs into the building.

"You're welcome!" you shout at his departing back, but the sarcasm doesn't seem to make a dent.

Quickly you scan the skies for the Vulture, but he has disappeared. The fact that your spider-sense has finally stopped tingling confirms this to you. With a sigh, you go to find MJ.

GO TO PAGE 80.

A s you stand there with your hand on the doorknob you can feel the seconds ticking away.

"Hurry up!" Alvarez whispers. "The bomb is right inside."

Still, you don't move. How did Alvarez and Markham find the bomb so quickly? And how do they know their way around the hallways of Madison Square Garden so well?

Your spider-sense is buzzing very strongly and you just *know* that it's warning you about something that is in the hallway with you, not whatever is on the other side of that door. Suddenly, you realize what is happening.

You turn back to face the door, and start to turn the knob. But instead of opening it, you place both hands on the door and kick backward with both feet, like a crazed mule. With a satisfying impact, you feel your boots connect with Alvarez and Markham, sending them both flying to the ground. An instant later you're hanging upside down, sending globs of webbing over the movie director and the special-effects man.

"No!" Markham cries. "You said you were one of the good guys!"

"I am," you reply. "I'm just not one of those really *dumb* good guys. Not dumb enough to be fooled by you—Mysterio!"

"Let us go!" Alvarez screams. "You're crazy."

"Come on, Chameleon," you say, satisfied that they are firmly tied. "This is getting a little old, don't you think?"

Markham and Alvarez freeze for a moment, and then suddenly their faces begin to shift and change. A moment later you see them in their real forms—Mysterio and the Chameleon.

"I should have known it all along," you say. "By taking over this movie, you could go anywhere in New York City you wanted without making people suspicious. You even got them to turn over Madison Square Garden."

You leave them tied up and hanging from the ceiling. By now you've figured out what's on the other side of the door—it leads back to the arena where the rest of the Sinister Six are waiting.

"I think I'll keep them waiting for a while," you say as you run in the other direction.

Minutes later, you're hanging from the ceiling of the arena again. Down below, the actors and film crew have been herded into seats. Doc Ock and the Shocker are standing by a doorway, waiting to spring the trap that the Chameleon and Mysterio were leading you to. Hobgoblin and the Vulture circle overhead.

Well, I guess they've waited long enough, you think. For the first time, you're beginning to feel like things are going your way. Without another thought you let go of the steel girder and drop straight down, free-falling through the air toward the ice, which rushes up from below. But you never hit the ice because you've timed your fall perfectly and strike the Vulture right between the shoulder blades as he flies by. You plummet down on top of him, driving him toward the floor. Only at the last second, when he has no chance to recover, do you shoot out a webline and swing away.

THWACK!

The Vulture hits the ground with a terrible crunching sound and he's out of commission.

"Look, It's him!" the Hobgoblin shouts from up above and he guns his glider toward you.

The Shocker and Doc Ock turn around in time to see the Hobgoblin's bomb miss you and strike the ice.

"I told you, Octopus!" the Shocker yells in frustration. "We should have destroyed him when we had the chance. Your fancy plans have gone bust again!"

"Don't panic, you fool!" the Hobgoblin screams, as he flies toward you.

You twist in midair, avoiding one of the Hobgoblin's razor-bats. You've got him on one side, the Shocker down below you and Doc Ock standing at the far side of the arena. You're making up your mind when you see the multi-armed villain turn suddenly and make a break for one of the exits.

He's giving up, you realize. He's leaving the Shocker and the Hobgoblin to hold me off while he tries to escape. I can't let him get away now!

Hobgoblin is circling and the Shocker is screaming at you from the floor. Neither of them has seen Doc Ock leave.

IF YOU FOLLOW DOC OCK,
GO TO PAGE 82.

IF YOU STAY TO FIGHT HOBGOBLIN AND
THE VULTURE, GO TO PAGE 87.

guess it's up to me, you sigh. This is probably a trap, you think as you start to climb.
But what else can I do? It's not like I can
sneak up on them or anything.

Trying to stay alert, you easily climb the
stones of the bridge tower. Still no sign of
anyone or anything, except for Mason. He's
strapped to a steel cable and titled over the
edge so he has to look straight down at the
terrifying drop. As soon as he sees you coming he starts screaming in fear.

"Stay away from me! Help! He's going to
kill me!"

You wince as you imagine what that
sounds like on television.

"Keep your shirt on, buddy," you call up
to him. "I'm here to save you. You know,
like the cavalry?"

"But Doctor Octopus said you were going
to come and kill me," Mason says.

"Well, don't believe everything you hear,"
you say as you haul yourself up to the top of

the tower. Now you're beside Mason but there's still no sign of the Six. But your spider-sense is buzzing, even though you can't see a cause for it. Quickly, you set Mason free and place him safely on the middle of the tower.

"Please," he pants. "I have to rest."

"Not here," you answer. "I have to get you down before the Sinister Six show up. They have something planned, I know."

"Just one minute," Mason pleads.

"I'll carry you," you say and you bend down to pick him up. As you do, the warning from your spider-sense gets even stronger. You look around quickly, but still you see nothing.

"Did you see where they went?" you ask.

"Yes," Mason says, his voice weak. You bend closer to hear him.

You see the needle coming toward you just a split second after your spider-sense gives you the warning. Caught off guard, you manage to twist away. The point stabs you below your shoulder, but doesn't go in very far.

"Not a deadly poison, you dimwit," Mason sneers. "Just something to make you safe and pliable while we go through our little play-acting."

"You're not Mason," you say as you drop to your knees.

"Of course not," he replies. "Only a fool like you would need a needle in his arm to figure it out. I'm the Chameleon, of course.

figure it out. I'm the Chameleon, of course. There never *was* a Mason. It's been *me* the whole time."

He grabs your hands and hauls you to your feet. "Ready for our big scene?" he says. He places your hands around his neck.

"Stop!" he screams. "Spider-Man, you're killing me!"

The crowd below roars in protest and fear. You want to break free but you can barely stand without the Chameleon's help. But the drug seems to be wearing off quickly.

Summoning all your strength, you break free and deliver a one-two punch to his head and body. The Chameleon goes down.

Shaking your head to fight off the dizziness, you bind him with some webbing, then collapse next to him. Unconscious, the Chameleon quickly shifts back to his true form. You stagger to your feet, holding his limp body. A few seconds later a rumble of voices sweeps through the crowd below. As you hoped, they've seen the transformation through the lenses of the television cameras.

Through the dim fog of the drugs in your brain, your spider-sense warns you of approaching danger. The Hobgoblin is flying toward you on his jet-glider and the Vulture is right behind him, soaring on his huge wings.

"Got to fight," you say, and stumble to the edge of the tower, getting ready to launch yourself into space. But the effect of the drug is still too strong. You fall forward off the tower and plunge straight down. Only instinct guides your web-shooter to send out a lifeline that stops your fall just as you hit the water below. Half senseless, you feel strong helping hands pull you from the cold waters of the river. Then everything goes black.

When you come to, you are lying on an ambulance gurney surrounded by concerned faces. "Chameleon!" you shout trying to leap up, but friendly hands push you back down.

"He got away," says a police captain. "They all did. But we got it all on video. Everyone knows you were being set up by them."

"I let them get away," you say to no one in particular.

That night, back at your apartment, you say the same thing to Mary Jane.

"That's all right, Tiger," she says giving you her thousand watt smile. "You win some, you lose some. At least their plot failed. The whole city knows you're still one of the good guys. I bet if you wanted to, *you* could run for Mayor."

"No thanks," you say with a grin. "The only thing I'm running for is a good night's sleep!"

THE END

I hope they know what they're doing, you say to yourself. Because that stunt sure *looks* dangerous.

In this scene, Mary Jane's character is supposed to sneak up on the movie bad guys by sliding along a wire from the balcony to the Trump Tower. You know that Mary Jane is only supposed to grab onto the wire. Then a stuntwoman, dressed in exactly the same clothes as MJ, will do the actual slide from building to building.

Mary Jane, the stuntwoman and Chip Alvarez are all standing near the edge of the balcony, talking to another man.

"Who's that?" you ask one of the crew members.

"That's Al Markham," he replies. "He's the special-effects director. The stunt coordinator is in charge of this stunt, but Al's got to make it look even more dangerous, using some movie magic."

"It seems dangerous enough," you say.

76

"It only *looks* dangerous," the man answers. " The stunt double will be clipped onto the wire with a safety line."

But in spite of his words, you can't relax. Your spider-sense is still buzzing.

Just then, in the street below you hear the sounds of sirens going by—real sirens, not movie ones.

"Hey, maybe they're after *real* terrorists," says a crew member.

"Wouldn't that be something?" you say, trying to laugh. But inside you're not laughing. Maybe those cops are heading for real trouble, you say to yourself. Maybe that's what my spider-sense was warning me about. But no, it can't be that. It only warns me about things that are close by.

Besides, those cops might not be going to an emergency. You can't make up your mind. Should you follow the police cars or stay with MJ?

IF YOU STAY, GO TO PAGE 131.

IF YOU GO TO THE CRIME SCENE, GO TO PAGE 134.

It's just as risky to try to lead the Shocker away, you think. Plus, where am I going to find an empty spot to fight him in midtown Manhattan during lunch hour?

You drop down to the sidewalk, trying to move too quickly for the Shocker. If you can get a little closer, you can get your webbing around his arms and shut down his blasters. You're almost there, just as another sonic blast shoots overhead. With a tremendous roar it smashes into the side of the bank, collapsing it inward.

"The hostages!" you cry.

"So long, Spider-Man!" the Shocker laughs and runs off, blasting his way through the police lines.

You're angry, but you don't have time to worry about the Shocker now. The whole front of the bank building is a pile of rubble. You can hear the screams of the hostages trapped inside. Working like a madman, you heave chunks of brick and concrete out of the way, lifting steel beams like they were twigs. Soon you reach the hostages. Luckily, the corner of the bank they were in did not collapse completely. They're all alive, but some have injuries.

"How could you let him do that?" the police captain asks you as the last of the injured are loaded into an ambulance.

"How could I . . ." you start to argue, but your heart isn't in it.

Just then a reporter from a local television station rushes up and shoves a microphone in your face.

"Spider-Man," she asks breathlessly, "is it true that you let the Shocker get away with three million dollars in cash? Is it true that several of the hostages were seriously injured? How does that make you feel, Spider-Man?"

Without saying a word, you turn and walk away. The truth is, it makes you feel like crying. "I don't think I can take it any more," you finally say out loud. "I don't want this responsibility. I want out." You resolve right then and there to give up being Spider-Man—and this time, forever.

END

"**D**on't sweat it," MJ says soothingly. "Tomorrow is another day, Tiger."

It's late at night and you've just finished venting a little frustration at all the crazy things that have happened to you in the past two days.

"Speaking of tomorrow," Mary Jane says, "since shooting of the movie is suspended, Alvarez has planned a cast party. With everything that's happened, he thinks we need a little morale booster. And maybe you could use one, too. Why don't you come along?"

IF YOU GO TO THE PARTY AS PETER PARKER, GO TO PAGE 29.

IF YOU GO PATROLLING THE CITY AS SPIDER-MAN, GO TO PAGE 19.

That guy is a kook, you say to yourself, but he's not my problem. It's these super baddies who I should be looking for.

You make it all the way to Greenwich Village without seeing so much as a jay-walker.

Pulling yourself upright, you stretch and peer up into the darkness. You catch a glimpse of a winged shape disappearing over a nearby rooftop. It's the Vulture! You swing up to the roof and begin to follow him.

He soars along at an easy pace. Soon he comes to a large, dark opening and enters.

That's the entrance to the abandoned East Side subway tunnel, you realize. Soundlessly, you creep inside.

GO TO PAGE 51.

The Shocker turns around and stands, dumbfounded, looking for Doc Ock, just as you swing overhead. You manage to drop a web-net over him without breaking your speed.

Maybe that will hold him, you think, as you drop to the ice and run out of the exit. Hobgoblin has already disappeared.

He could be halfway to New Jersey by now, you think. But I have to find Doc Ock, because if I know him, he hasn't really left— he's gone to set off that bomb.

Moving faster than you ever have, you catch a glimpse of Doc Ock's strange spiderlike form as it disappears into an elevator. He's heading for the roof, you realize. I have to beat him there, or at least hitch a ride.

You run to the elevator door, go to the one next to it and with a tremendous heave, yank open the steel doors.

"Going up!" you shout, as you send a web-line to the elevator car, climbing gently up after it. There are four elevator shafts in a row, so you have room to climb and in no time you've standing on top of Ock's car. As the elevator comes to a stop, you kick in the escape panel in the car's roof.

"Top floor," you say. "Shoes, appliances—and your friendly neighborhood Spider-Man!"

You shoot a glob of webbing right at Doc Ock's eyes. Blinded, he lashes out furiously, sending two of his steel arms crashing through the roof of the elevator. You avoid the steel claws, but you can't get past them.

Then, in a flash, they're gone and Ock has left the elevator. You're right on his heels. He leads you down a hallway and you see that you're both in the ceiling of the Garden, over the arena. Above you are stairs leading to the roof of the building.

"Give it up, Ock!" you yell.

He turns and glares at you.

"You may have panicked those fools," he says. "But not Doctor Octopus. I'm not fleeing you, Spider-Man. I was running—to this!"

One of his steel arms reaches up into the bundle of pipes running overhead and pulls out a small black box.

"Stop where you are!" he commands. "This is the controller for the bomb under the seats below. One more step and I will set it off!"

"Okay Ock, I stopped," you say. "But

haven't you forgotten one thing? You're still here. You set off the bomb and you die, also."

"Not I, Spider-Menace," Doc gloats. "It's a radiation bomb, and we are far enough away now not to be affected. But all those below will be exposed to enough rads to make them die slow, horrible deaths."

"Okay, Doc, " you say with a sigh. "You win. What do you want? You going to boil me in oil or just make me watch your home videos?"

"We will see," Doc Ock gloats. "Right now you will come with me—and no tricks or I set off the bomb."

Ock points to the stairs leading to the roof and reluctantly you start to climb them. You hear him following you.

"I've done it!" Doc Ock is babbling to himself. "And without the help of those incompetent fools. I never needed them at all!"

Suddenly you flip backward, toward the claw that is holding the bomb switch. Doc Ock, lost in his dream of victory, is just a fraction of a second too slow. You kick the box free and it goes clattering down the steps.

"Gee, too bad, Ock," you say, landing behind him. "You really oughta be more careful."

"No!" Ock screams. He stands there frozen for a moment and then turns and runs up the stairs. The next thing you know, you're thrown backward by the force of a small explosion. Ock has set off a booby trap. You get up and run through the smoke, coming out on the roof just in time to see Ock climb into a waiting helicopter. As the chopper lifts off, you snag it with a web-line.

You rise through the air, dangling from the chopper's struts. As you climb up your webbing, the helicopter banks and heads out toward the Hudson River. Before long you have crawled to the front of the aircraft and you raise yourself up to the windshield. There is Ock, piloting the machine.

You can't hear Ock over the roar of the blades, but his face turns red and his mouth opens in a scream. Without thinking, he plunges two of his claws through the windshield, trying to grab you. You drop out of the way, firmly anchored to the helicopter with a web-line. The wind rushes in and pins Ock backward. As it does he loses control of the chopper.

You can see him bellow in anger. Doc Ock shakes his human fist at you and his claws reach out. In his madness, he is destroying the helicopter.

With a final furious roar, his steel arms come snatching for you. One steely arm wildly hits the rotor blades with a tremendous shriek of metal on metal. Another brushes you, knocking you into the air. You begin to fall. Using years of practice, you weave together a parachute and use it to break your fall. You float down gently as Ock's helicopter falls like a stone into the waters of the harbor below. The last you see of him is a glint of four steel arms waving at you. Then it hits the water with a mighty blast and disappears.

Later, much later, you are finally back at home with MJ.

"You did it, Peter," she says. "You defeated the Sinister Six and got your reputation back."

"I did, didn't I?" you say, feeling relieved for the first time.

"You're a hero again," MJ says with a broad smile. "And now that the police have found the real Chip Alvarez, the movie can continue. I think they should write in a part for Spider-Man."

"No thanks," you laugh. "The only way I want to see movies from now on is in a theater with a big box of popcorn."

THE END

've got to get these people to safety, you think with regret. I can't go off after Doc Ock now.

You catch a last glimpse of Doc Ock vanishing out the door. But your spider-sense warns you that the Hobgoblin is gunning his glider for you.

"This battle, this arena, will be your last!" he screams, his demonic mask twisted in rage. You swing sideways, flip over in the air and send a web-line shooting out. You just miss the villain, but the line catches the edge of his glider. It tilts it just enough to throw the Hobgoblin off balance.

You drop from your perch, using your weight to tip the glider even more. The Hobgoblin screeches and falls, grabbing the edge of the glider with his gloved hands.

"Shocker, what are you doing here?" you yell as you drop, pulling the glider with you. "Even Ock had enough sense to run by now."

The Hobgoblin falls, striking the ice just

a few feet from the Shocker. The Shocker's moment of indecision is all that you need. You drop straight toward him, shooting a wide spray of webbing. By the time he sees you and tries to raise his vibro-blasters, it's too late—he's completely trapped. Just to make sure, you land squarely on him, knocking him to the floor in a heap. In no time at all you've securely bound him and the Hobgoblin, too.

The hundreds of actors and movie people in the stands cheer you wildly. But you have no time to congratulate yourself.

"Quick, everybody!" you shout over the din. "Get up and follow me!"

You swing over the crowd and search for Mary Jane. There she is, helping one of the injured actors up the stairs. You drop down.

"Let me help you with that, ma'am," you say, giving her arm a knowing squeeze.

Carefully slinging the injured man over your shoulder, you swing away, and lead the crowd to the nearest emergency exit.

Remembering what Ock said about booby traps, you shout, "Stand back, everyone!" Taking a deep breath, you kick the door open. Nothing happens.

"Everyone out!" you yell. Handing over the injured actor you wait until MJ and everyone else is clear of the building. Then you follow them into the warm sunshine, where about a hundred policemen are waiting.

"There he is!" one of them shouts. "It's Spider-Man! He stopped the Sinister Six!"

The crowd cheers. Now you know that it really is over—you did stop them and, better yet, you're a hero again to the people of New York.

"I was just glad to get everyone out," you say later, giving an interview as Spider-Man to a local television reporter. "I was worried about the bomb Doctor Octopus mentioned."

"You didn't know there was no bomb?" the reporter asks.

"No," you say. "We only found that out later."

MJ steps up to the camera. "As an innocent bystander," she says with a big grin, "let me just say that after seeing Spider-Man in action today I don't think the people of New York have anything to worry about."

As the crowd cheers wildly, you just stand there and soak it up. You know, you think to yourself, sometimes, this super hero biz isn't too bad.

THE END

"It's a good thing I talked to that special-effects assistant," you say to yourself. "That's how I know those squibs are tiny explosives. If I can set them off, Ock will think someone is shooting at him. That might be all the break I need."

Without another moment's thought, you tumble sideways, throwing yourself onto the ice. Chameleon and Mysterio were guarding against you charging Doc Ock, but none of them expected you to move *away* from him. This gives you the extra few seconds you need to slide across the ice, snag the controls and hit the button with your elbow. At the same time you shout in your loudest voice: "Take cover!"

At that moment the squibs go off, sounding like a machine gun and tearing up the ice at Doc Ock's feet. The Vulture and the Hobgoblin fly in circles, panicked, looking for the gunman. The Shocker runs to take cover. Startled, Doc Ock drops the controls for your shackles and you feel them loosen.

"That's all the room I need," you say, and with a mighty pull you tear yourself free of them.

The Sinister Six are still in a state of confusion. You're moving too fast for them. But Ock still has MJ in his grasp. You shoot a line of webbing around his knees and yank him onto the ice. This makes him release MJ, who hits the floor, stunned, but unhurt. In a flash, you're at her side.

"Sorry to do this, MJ," you whisper to her. "But I have to get you out of here, fast."

She gives you a brave smile, then a second later you are sending her sliding across the ice like a giant red-headed hockey puck. You watch as she hits the side boards, jumps to her feet and climbs safely out of the rink.

You twist around. You know Octopus is the key.

If I can get some more webbing on Ock, he'll be out of the way, then the rest of this gang will collapse, you think. But it's too late. The rest of the Sinister Six have recovered and they're coming at you from all sides. One of Hobgoblin's bombs explodes just inches away from you as you leap out of the way, swinging across the ice on a web-line. Smoke from the explosion blows across the rink and you see a chance. You release the line, shoot out another one, turn in mid-air and land with both feet on the Shocker, flattening him like a pancake. In a flash, you have him web-tied hand and foot and you shoot him across the ice into the goal at the other end. The buzzer sounds and the red light flashes.

"A goal!" you shout, and to your relief, the crowd of actors and extras in the stands cheers for you.

The Vulture is coming in like a dive bomber. You tumble out of the way, shoot a web-line to one of the giant video screens overhead and swing up into the rafters. Now you have plenty of room to maneuver along the beams in the ceiling and Doc Ock can't reach you with his arms.

You lower yourself on a web-line until you're hanging in mid-air.

"Come on, Hobby!" you taunt the Hobgoblin. He guns his jet-glider at you as the Vulture flies toward you from another direction. You swing around, letting them get closer, pretending you don't see the danger— but actually you want to time things just right, so that . . .

"Watch out, fool!" the Hobgoblin cries. But it's too late.

WHAM!

You did it. You led the Hobgoblin right into the oncoming Vulture, sending him crashing to the ground. The Hobgoblin veers off, barely recovering. Meanwhile, you drop toward the ice like a stone, hitting the Vulture and webbing him up before he can recover.

92

The Hobgoblin screams in anger! "You will not win!" he shouts.

"That's what I like," you reply. "Positive thinking."

The villain roars and sends his glider flying at you. But in the crash with the Vulture it must have been damaged, because it tilts badly and the Hobgoblins spills out in midair.

A moment later, the Hobgoblin is wrapped up in webbing and out of the fight. Now Doc Ock is moving toward you. The Chameleon is out of sight. You're trying to make up your mind who to take on next when a sound from the stands whips your head around.

The hundreds of extras are jumping out of their seats and running for the exits again. They're terrified because it looks like dozens of masked, black-suited terrorists are firing into the stands with machine guns.

"It can't be," you say to yourself. "They're not real." You realize that it's a trick of Mysterio.

The crowd is in no real danger. But some of them might get hurt in the panic. What should you do?

IF YOU TRY TO STOP THE PANIC,
GO TO PAGE 58.

IF YOU KEEP FIGHTING,
GO TO PAGE 62.

don't see why the Sinister Six would attack that movie set again, you think. They seem to have bigger fish to fry.

You've already said goodbye to Mary Jane and you're about to head to the roof when you hear another news bulletin come over the radio.

"We have this just in. True to their word, the gang of criminals calling itself the Sinister Six has struck. They've kidnapped the outspoken candidate for mayor, Bob Mason. Just minutes ago, the kidnappers released this tape, which is apparently that of Mason himself pleading for his release."

You hear Mason's terrified voice issuing from your radio.

"Help me, please! These madmen are going to kill me. They all hate me because of the way I've spoken out against them. Especially Spider-Man. Help me, please!"

The voice on the radio is cut off suddenly and replaced by another. To your shock, it's your own!

"This is Spider-Man. Unless the mayor delivers twenty million dollars in ransom to us by 10 A.M. today, Bob Mason will die. And he'll just be the first. Many more will suffer if you dare to defy us."

You stand rooted to the spot, overcome by anger and revulsion. The whole city just heard you threaten to kill someone. Or at least, that's what they're going to *think* they heard.

The radio announcer continues.

"That's all we know so far. There are reports that the police have closed all the approaches to the Brooklyn Bridge, and that this is the location at which Spider-Man is holding Mason captive."

You don't wait to hear more. You're already out over the street, heading for the Brooklyn Bridge. You arrive minutes later, having hitched a ride on the top of a police van that was speeding to the scene.

The area around the Brooklyn Bridge is a chaotic mass of police cars, vans, fire trucks television crews and crowds of people. You spring for a van as it pulls to a stop and swing over to a nearby building, hiding in the shadows. At the top of the bridge tower nearest Manhattan you see a small figure strapped to a support cable. You can't see clearly from where you are, but you're sure it's Mason. There's no sign of the Sinister Six.

Here I go again, you think, swinging from

your safe perch on the building toward the bridge.

The crowd below soon spots you and their shouts and screams of fear tell you how many of them believe what they've recently heard about you.

Great! you think as you swing toward the old granite and stone bridge tower. I show up and everyone thinks I'm the bad guy. This doesn't exactly make me feel welcome.

You swing upward and land on one of the many cables that hold up the bridge. Now you can see Mason clearly. He looks small and pitiful, hanging near the edge of that steep drop. You know there's no way the police can deliver that ransom money in time, even if they wanted to. It looks like it's up to you to save the politician, if you can. What do you do?

IF YOU DECIDE TO SAVE MASON,
GO TO PAGE 72.

IF YOU DECIDE NOT TO RESCUE HIM,
GO TO PAGE 108.

I must sense the bomb inside, you tell yourself. Better get in there and take care of it. Bracing yourself, you carefully open the door and step inside.

As soon as you do, you realize you've made a mistake. You've walked right out to the edge of the hockey rink and four members of the Sinister Six are waiting for you: the Shocker, Hobgoblin, the Vulture and Doc Octopus.

But Markham and Alvarez ... you begin to think just as Alvarez runs past you.

"Watch out!" he shouts. "We opened the wrong door!" You reach out to stop him. Everything starts happening at once. Alvarez turns, and with an evil grin whips a strange shiny device out from under his jacket. From behind, you sense Markham running at you. And directly ahead are the four evil-looking claws of Doctor Octopus, snaking their way toward you at lightning speed. You're caught completely off guard, and before even you can react, Alvarez has snapped a strange device over your hands while from behind Markham as done the same to your legs.

But, of course, by now you know they're not Alvarez and Markham. With a sickening thud in the pit of you stomach it hits you—you've been tricked. It comes as no surprise when Markham and Alvarez vanish and you find yourself face to face with Mysterio and the Chameleon!

"You lousy . . ." you begin to sputter. Driven into a rage, you strain against the shackles on your hands and legs until your muscles feel like they're about to burst but the steel manacles don't budge a centimeter.

"Go ahead, Spider-Monkey," sneers the Shocker. "Bust a gut. You'll never break out of those handcuffs."

"He's right, of course," says Doc Ock. One of his steel claws hovers just inches from your face. "They've been designed by me, so naturally they're unbreakable. Are they a little too tight? Perhaps I can adjust them."

You watch as Ock fiddles with a small box he holds in his two human hands. Instantly the steel cuffs on your hands and legs tighten and an electric shock shoots through your body.

"Arrgh!" you scream in pain.

"Sorry," Ock says, taking his hand off the control. "That was a little *too* tight, wasn't it?" Then, in a different tone, he adds, "Bring him to me!"

Mysterio and the Chameleon shove you onto the ice and toward Doc Ock. He waits in the middle of the lights, boxes and coiled cables set up by the movie crew. In spite of your rage, you try to keep calm, taking in every detail. You see that most of the extras and actors have been herded into the seats lining the hockey rink. All the props, cameras and other equipment for the shoot lie strewn about where it was dropped in the panic. Then you notice that Ock is standing right on top of some squibs that were dropped by one of the special-effects assistants. Carefully you search the stands for a sign of MJ but you can't pick her out.

You turn to the Chameleon. "You've been Alvarez all along, haven't you?"

The answers comes from his spooky, featureless face. "That's right," he says. "The real Alvarez is safely out of the way. The same for the real Al Markham."

"Who was replaced by Mysterio," you interject. "Of course. With his background in special effects, it was easy."

"Too easy," Mysterio sneers. "My talent is wasted on a ridiculous thriller like this one."

Through the pain you realize why your spider-sense seemed to be acting funny. It was warning you about Alvarez and Markham.

But you kept thinking it was warning you about something else.

"The movie allowed us to move around New York freely," says Doc Ock. "It gave us access to places like this wonderful arena and all these lovely hostages. And it gave us a way to attract Spider-Man's friends. Peter Parker and his lovely wife. Let's give her a hand! Or should I say, a claw?"

You can barely breathe as one of Ock's claws snakes behind some crates and comes out holding MJ tightly in its grip.

"Here is our beautiful star now," he gloats, handling her almost as if she were a doll. "As I have said, Spider-Man, we don't wish merely to destroy you—we want you to suffer. That's why we're not going to kill you today. We *are* going to blow up this arena. The police, who are already outside, will rush in and who will they find surrounded by the evidence—Spider-Man. Yes, Spider-Man, you will be blamed for the death and destruction we cause today."

"Stop it!" MJ screams. "You're hurting me!"

You can only stand by helplessly, although every muscle in your body is straining to go to MJ's rescue.

"But first, Spider-Menace," Ock continues, "you will suffer even more. We had hoped to reward you with the death of your friend, Peter Parker. But he seems to have run off like a coward. We will have to make do with a, how do the movie people put this—a stand-in. And here she is."

He shakes MJ back and forth. You can see the terror on her face as she bravely tries to hold herself together.

"Let her go, Ock!" you shout. "This is between you and me!"

"Suffering already, are you?" Ock gloats. "Very good. That's what we want to see."

There must be something I can do, you think. Your hands and feet are tightly bound. But the cuffs seem to be radio controlled. Ock is holding the controller in his human hands, not his claws. If you can just get there fast enough, you might be able to knock the controls out of his hands and get free. Once again, your eyes rest on the squibs Doc Ock is standing on. You see their remote control device. It's only a few feet away, between you and the Chameleon. You remember one of the special-effects people telling you how they work. Can they help you somehow?

That's your choice: To make a break for Doc Ock, or try to activate the squibs. Your time is running out.

IF YOU ATTACK DOC OCK AND TRY TO SAVE MJ, GO TO PAGE 38.

IF YOU TRY TO USE THE SPECIAL-EFFECTS EQUIPMENT, GO TO PAGE 90.

She's about to drop, you think. I'd better get to her—fast!

And in the split second it takes you to make that decision, her lifeline snaps! As if everything's in slow motion, you can see her begin to fall to the street, hundreds of feet below.

Adjusting your swing, you aim to head off her fall and catch her. Then, in the next split second, you're right below the stuntwoman— but she's gone! In fact, in the blink of an eye, the entire scene has changed. The stuntwoman is still hanging from the cable, only now she's behind you. Somehow, you've turned completely around and you're headed back toward the building you started from. And the stone wall is coming at you like a freight train! Only a lightning-fast twist saves you from crashing into it head-first.

What happened? How could you make such a mistake? Someone or something is playing tricks on you.

"Spider-Man, what are you doing?" It's Chip Alvarez, the director, shouting at you from the balcony, a few feet away. He looks furious. "How can you play games at a time like this? Why don't you rescue her?"

You realize that to Alvarez and everyone else, it looks like you're swinging around, ignoring the danger to the stunt woman. You've got to rescue her. But how? Something created an illusion, making you almost crash headfirst into the side of the building. You would have, too, if your spider-sense hadn't warned you. And your spider-sense is still tingling. How do you know that you're not seeing an illusion now?

IF YOU TRY TO SAVE THE
STUNTWOMAN, GO TO PAGE 42.

IF YOU LOOK FOR THE CAUSE OF THE
ILLUSION, GO TO PAGE 40.

Got to stay by MJ, you think, your mind reeling. But what is making me feel like this?

"C'mon, Parker," Markham says kindly. "Come out and get some fresh air."

"No," you say, "I just need something to drink."

You shake loose of his grip and try to force your way back to Mary Jane. Your spider-sense is buzzing all the time, but your head seems a little clearer. When you reach her, you lean over and whisper, "Something's wrong. I think we'd better get out of here."

"Are you sure?" she asks. "You've been a little jumpy."

"No, it's my spider-sense," you reply. "I know that—"

BAROOM!

Like a shock wave from an earthquake, the floor of the ballroom begins to shake.

"What is it?" someone yells.

You know what it is—the Shocker. You

just have time to grab MJ and push her toward an exit before the crowd starts to panic. Then the brown-and-yellow suited villain bursts through a window, riding a large floating glider that looks suspiciously like the kind the Hobgoblin rides.

MJ disappears out the exit, forced on by the rushing mass of people. You turn, feeling helpless without your spider-suit on.

"You, Parker!" the Shocker calls out. "Don't move and no one will get hurt."

You have no choice but to obey him.

He strolls closer, sneering beneath his mask.

At least MJ is out of here, you think. But much to your surprise you see her walk back into the room.

"MJ, get out of here," you start to cry. But she stops you with a sickly grin.

"Why, Peter, aren't you glad to see me?" It's Mary Jane's mouth, but her voice is someone else's. Horrified, you watch as her features begin to shift and dissolve. In a few moments Mary Jane's face has been transformed into the white, featureless mask of the Chameleon.

"Yes, Parker, it's not your lovely wife," the Chameleon gloats. "But think of how easy it would be for me to get to her."

"Why, you!" your rage almost gets the better of you, but you manage to restrain yourself.

Parker," the Chameleon says. "It's Spider-Man we want. Spider-Man owes us—he owes me for pain, humiliation, failure. We know you can get to him. You tell him this: Either he shows up where and when we tell him to, or you and your lovely wife will be . . . well, let us say it won't be pretty."

"He won't do—" you start to protest. But the Chameleon interrupts.

"Now, now," he says. "I'm sure you can persuade him. We'll be in touch."

With a terrible laugh, the Chameleon turns his back on you and strolls to the balcony.

"So long, sucker," the Shocker scoffs and follows him. You can only stand frozen to the spot as they both mount the glider and take off into the night sky.

Your rage and anger make you want to go running after them, track them down and put them where they can never hurt MJ or anyone. They don't know that you're Spider-Man. Should you follow them or stay with MJ?

IF YOU FOLLOW THEM,
GO TO PAGE 57.

IF YOU STAY WITH MJ,
GO TO PAGE 56.

Mason is connected to all the trouble I've been having, you tell yourself. I just know it.

You swing crosstown to the television studios. After what seems like hours, you see him emerge from the building, get in his waiting car and zoom off. Unfortunately, he doesn't lead you anywhere too exciting. Finally, in the early hours of the morning you follow him back to his apartment, where, as near as you can tell, he goes to sleep.

Cold, tired and hungry, you tumble into your apartment where MJ is waiting, already in bed.

GO TO PAGE 136.

Me, save Mason? They have to be kidding, you think. You practically bound up the side of the bridge tower, knowing exactly what you're gong to do. Mason screams in fear as you get closer.

"Don't kill me, Spider-Man!" he screams

"Don't worry, I won't kill you," you say, climbing onto the top of the tower. "I just want to make you a little more comfortable."

You raise both arms and send powerful jets of webbing around the politicians arms and legs.

"What are you doing?" he yells.

"Just making sure you're really tied up," you reply. "Mr. Mason. Or should I say, Chameleon!"

"You're nuts!" he yells.

"Am I?" you answer, and faster than the eye can follow, your right fist shoots out and cracks Mason in the jaw. He blacks out and, as you knew it would, the face of Mason quickly transforms back into the head of the Chameleon.

108

"Lucky thing I overheard him and Doc Ock talking about their plan back in that subway tunnel," you say to yourself. But you don't have time to celebrate. The Hobgoblin on his glider, the Vulture winging his way over the East River, and the Shocker, Doc Ock and Mysterio flying on some kind of jet helicopter, are all headed toward you in the sky over the Bridge.

The first to reach you is the Vulture.

"Wait!" you hear Doc Ock's amplified voice cry out through the air. "Attack as a team!"

"The Vulture doesn't need a team!" the green-suited maniac replies. "I deserve the glory of bringing Spider-Man to his knees."

Distracted by his argument with Doc Ock, the Vulture has let his guard down. He swoops too close to the bridge as you swing out toward him, connecting with both feet in his midsection.

"Help!" he screams, losing control and beginning to fall.

You pull him back with you as you swing toward the bridge again. The stunned Vulture finds himself tied with webbing to one of the bridge cables.

"You fool!" It's the Hobgoblin, riding in on his glider. He's screaming at the Vulture. "We told you to wait. Now watch how a true fighter dispatches Spider-Man!"

Two pumpkin bombs head for you, one on either side. You simply let go of your hold on the bridge and drop. You feel the heat of the bombs exploding above as you swing yourself completely under the bridge. Your spider-sense tells you that the Hobgoblin is following you. A second later, one of his razor-bats slices through your web-line.

The Hobgoblin zooms under the bridge, yelling triumphantly.

"He's down!" the criminal shouts. "He fell! Now he's mine!"

As the glider emerges on the other side of the bridge, you look down from the cable you're clinging to.

"Wait . . ." you tell yourself. "Wait for it. Now!"

You drop on the Hobgoblin as his jet-glider passes underneath. Your fists lash out like jackhammers, striking the villain's gruesome mask over and over. With one last blow, you drive him off the glider.

"Noo!" he screams.

"Yess!" you reply as you stop his fall with a web-net. In a matter of seconds he is also firmly bound and hanging from the bridge.

The next thing you know your reflexes have made you jump sideways as a vibro-blast from the Shocker rips through the air where you were just standing. You race up, until you stand on one of the two great, curved cables that support the bridge. The helicopter swoops closer and the Shocker lets loose another blast.

Your weight is just enough to tilt the helicopter sideways as the Shocker aims another blast at you.

Suddenly the chopper dips down and disappears from view.

"Gee, where'd everybody go?" you call. A moment later it swings up from under the bridge on the other side. Then a second jet helicopter, also carrying Ock, Mysterio and the Shocker comes shooting up on your side of the span. Then a third appears in the air above you—and a fourth.

"They're multiplying like rabbits!" you shout in mock fear. You know this is a trick of Mysterio's. Only one of the jet choppers can be real.

"Oh my, oh my!" you shout. "Whatever shall I do?"

Standing absolutely still, you feel the cable you're standing on sway in a strong wind . . . a wind coming from behind you!

That's it! you think. That's how I know which is the real helicopter—it's the one creating gusts of wind with its propellers!

You flip around, fall through the air and swing backward.

"He's coming at us!" the real Shocker screams in panic.

"I see him, you fool!" Ock shouts back, yanking on the controls of the helicopter.

He reaches out with two of his steel arms to grab you, but you have no intention of getting that close. Instead, you hook one side of the helicopter with a web-line and let yourself drop straight down. Your weight is just enough to tilt the chopper sideways as the Shocker aims another blast at you. His shot goes wild and blasts through the roof of the helicopter, crumpling the blades. As you swing to safety you watch the machine plunge to the bridge below, a twisted, crumpled mess.

It doesn't take you long to drop down and tie up the three criminals, who are now in no condition to put up a fight.

"He did it!" the crowd cheers. It's just a few minutes later but now the entire bridge is packed with cheering, screaming people.

"I think the city owes you an apology, Spider-Man," says the police commissioner who has arrived at the scene. "Bob Mason was the Chameleon all along. We should have known that you'd never join a bunch of thugs like the Sinister Six."

"That's right," you say, beaming. "As long as I'm your friendly neighborhood Spider-Man, you can count on it!"

THE END

As much as I'd love to get that creep, I'd better make sure that stuntwoman is all right, you say to yourself as you watch Mysterio taunt you from the distant rooftop.

Flipping backward, you roll off the roof of the Trump Tower and free fall down the side of the skyscraper. There she is, exactly where you expected her to be. Mysterio seems to have disappeared, because you now have no trouble telling what's real and what isn't.

It's a good thing I came back, you think, breaking your fall with a web-line. You raise your arm in mid-flight to shoot a web under the stuntwoman, but at that very moment the end of her cable attached to the Trump Tower snaps. With a helpless feeling you watch her swing toward the side of the building across the street. Everything happens too fast for even you to react.

The stuntwoman plummets toward the side of the building, but then you see it—the movie crew has managed to get a net under her. She's caught in its folds, bruised but okay. You hurriedly swing over to make sure she's okay. Landing on the balcony, you walk over to where the cast and crew are crowded around.

"Thank goodness," you sigh.

"What are you doing here!" an angry voice demands.

It's Chip Alvarez, the director. "Haven't you had enough fun, playing around while she almost dropped to her death?"

Without a word, you flip off the balcony and disappear. With a heavy heart, you force yourself to change back into your Peter Parker clothes and rejoin Mary Jane. You're just in time to see Alvarez being interviewed for the local TV newscast.

"This so-called hero," he says angrily, "this Spider-Man, literally hung around while one of our crew nearly died. He's a disgrace!"

Barely containing your own anger, you whisper to Mary Jane, "I've got to get out of here."

"Okay, Peter," she says sadly and gives you a kiss on the cheek. Her look tells you that she knows you did the best you could.

GO TO PAGE 31.

You leap from the tunnel ceiling ready for a fight.

"It's him!" the Hobgoblin cries. "It's Spider-Man!" His jet-glider soars toward you. The Vulture is right behind him.

A pumpkin bomb hurtles toward you, striking the tunnel wall just feet away and exploding with a powerful blast. Luckily, you were ready for it and you roll with the power of the explosion, still heading for the glider.

You come up on your feet, standing stock still as the deadly machine rushes toward you. Then, at the very last moment, you spring upward and to the side, clinging to the tunnel wall.

"Arrgh!" the Hobgoblin screams in frustration as he roars past, colliding with the concrete wall.

But there's no time to celebrate because the Vulture is almost on top of you. You swing sideways on a web-line, then back, like a wild pendulum.

"Hold still!" the Vulture shouts. He's having trouble turning as his wings keep brushing the tunnel walls.

"Stop your—" the Vulture starts to say, but that's all he can manage, because he's now completely caught in the web you've made for him.

"I'm stuck!" he shouts in rage.

"Don't think of it as stuck," you answer. "Think of it as resting."

"Work together!" you hear Doc Ock roar as you barely escape the snapping claws of another arm that has appeared out of nowhere. Your strategy has worked so far. Two of the Sinister Six are out of action for the moment. But you now face Doc Ock, the Shocker, Mysterio and the Chameleon. The Hobgoblin and the Vulture are behind you— and they won't stay out of commission for long.

Almost on cue, one of the Hobgoblin's bombs goes whistling past, missing you thanks only to a warning from your spider-sense. It explodes right in front of the Shocker, knocking him backward and out of sight for the moment.

Somewhere behind you, the Hobgoblin has freed the Vulture, and the two of them attack you from the rear. The Vulture is flapping madly about like a crazed bat. The Hobgoblin, now on foot, is throwing bombs and razor-bats at you from every angle. The

Shocker recovers quickly and his blasts ring off the tunnel walls, until you're deaf from the echoes and debris from cracked and crumbling concrete begins to pile up.

The tide is beginning to turn against you. At one point, you almost lose your footing. You see two Shockers coming toward you at the same time. The other "Shocker" must be the Chameleon. Both are poised to blast you, both have a clear shot. Which way should you leap?

You jump to the right, avoiding the blast from the real Shocker, roll forward under one of Doc Ock's arms and deliver a knockout blow to the surprised Chameleon. Ducking under a razor-bat that bounces off the wall harmlessly, you shoot a line of webbing that snags the Shocker's legs. You yank back with all your might and he falls forward with a thud. In a flash, you're on him and have him bound tightly with webbing.

Two down! you think, and the tide begins to turn in your favor.

"Well, Ock, your team is working the way it usually does," you taunt him as you swing across the tunnel to get closer. "But I think you need a new name. How about the Six Stooges? You know, twice as stupid as the Three Stooges."

"You are the one who is lacking in intelligence," Ock gasps, working his arms furiously. "For now I have you in my clutches."

"Oh, really?" you say. Guided by your spider-sense, you swing away just as the Vulture swoops in toward you. Instead of catching you, Doc Ock's steel claws grab the Vulture in a violent embrace, throwing him to the floor. Once again, you're there in a flash and have him bound head and foot before he can recover.

Twisting sideways, you brace yourself for another attack by Ock's arms. But even as they draw near, they seem to vanish. Suddenly there are two steel rails running down the tunnel. And the vibrations in the walls and floor tell you one thing—this subway is running and there's a train coming straight for you.

You must jump aside or be crushed. Yet you know it's not possible—it must be one of Mysterio's tricks! Yet your spider-sense is tingling.

GO TO PAGE 36.

119

Confused and feeling weak, you let Markham lead you out onto the balcony. Your mind is fogged, but through the haze you think, I need to get out of this party. If there's any danger, I have to get ready to face it.

For a moment the cool night air does help a little, but your spider-sense is buzzing even stronger.

Suddenly it hits you—it's Markham, he's the source of the danger! You wheel to face him when MJ comes strolling out onto the balcony.

"MJ, what are you . . ." you begin, but then your voice trails off. For as you watch, MJ's lovely features dissolve into a white putty-like mask. And at the same time, Al Markham's face and body starts to shift and vibrate. Your head reels and you have to grab the railing to keep from collapsing.

Now you know the source of the dizzy feeling you have: Al Markham is really Mysterio, master of illusion! And that's not MJ, it's the

Chameleon! But what do they want with Peter Parker?

"Recognize us, Parker?" the Chameleon says, as if he can read your thoughts. "Try to concentrate. We're not after you—it's your friend, Spider-Man. We owe him a big debt, one that we're going to repay—and you're going to help us."

"But . . ." you try to protest, but the gas has you in its power.

"You're going to bring Spider-Man to a place we tell you," the Chameleon continues, his strange, featureless head only inches from yours. "And if you don't, you'll face the consequences. You *or* your lovely wife."

You try to speak, but you can't. Everything is getting darker.

"That's right," says Mysterio. "Go to sleep. We'll leave you a little token of what we're capable of. Just remember it's only a taste of what we'll do."

You reach out to grab him but the floor swims up at you and you're out cold.

When you come to, there's no sign of the Chameleon or Mysterio. Instead, dazed and shocked people line the walls. The place has been wrecked. You grab the nearest person, one of the men from the movie crew.

"What happened?" you ask.

"Some guy calling himself the Shocker," the man says. "He blew in and destroyed the place. Said it was a warning, but he didn't say for what."

"Anyone hurt?" you ask, still feeling dazed.

"Yes—" he says. But before he can finish his sentence your eyes have followed his gaze. With a cold rush of fear you realize the form lying on the ground surrounded by ambulance attendants is Mary Jane. You rush to her side. She's barely conscious but she recognizes you.

"She'll be okay," says one of the medics. "But she's badly hurt. They say the Shocker was *aiming* for her."

Numbly, you follow them as they rush MJ to the waiting ambulance.

This is my fault, you say to yourself over and over. If I wasn't Spider-Man . . . If I hadn't gone out onto that balcony . . . If only I had stayed by MJ.

I'm taking her far away from here, you vow. Where the Chameleon and Mysterio and the Shocker can never reach her. From now on, she's my number-one priority. Spider-Man has had it!

END

"You're going to bring Spider-Man to a place we tell you," the Chameleon continues. "And if you don't, you'll pay the consequences."

If there's going to be a brawl, why should I be the only one to have some fun? you think, as slowly you back your way along the ceiling. I'm pretty sure the Fantastic Four are in town. They can be here in a matter of minutes.

As you back away, Doc Ock's ranting grows fainter. Then you hear Ock say something that grabs your attention like nothing else he's said.

"Yes, that pitiful wall-crawler! Everywhere he goes he'll find people who hate him, people who want him arrested. And it's all thanks to our good friend Bob Mason. Mr. Mason, take a bow!"

Mason! Here? you freeze, waiting to hear more. Your eyes strain to find the figure of the politician, but you can't make him out. Then, to your surprise, you see the white mask of the Chameleon begin to shift and change. In seconds it has become the face of Bob Mason.

"Yes, I must say inventing Bob Mason was a stroke of genius, even though it was my own idea," Octopus raves.

A strange quiet falls across the long, dark tunnel as Doc Ock's mad laughter echoes in the distance. And in the quiet the smallest noise is magnified—like the sound of the scurrying rat, that leaps from a timber next to you, sending some bits of concrete falling to the floor. The tiny sound bounces off the curved walls until it reaches the Sinister Six, who as one turn to face in your direction.

"We have a visitor," Dr. Ock says in a calm, menacing voice. "Find out who it is."

In a flash, the Hobgoblin and the Vulture start flying down the tunnel straight toward you.

"Well, so much for evening the odds," you say as you rush to meet them.

GO TO PAGE 116.

I don't want to turn my back on Hobgoblin, you think. He might be using the actors and the bus as bait of some kind. My best bet is to wrap him up first.

You swing right toward him, flipping around to avoid another pumpkin bomb. This is almost too easy, you think, swinging in the other direction. Each arc brings you closer to the grinning Hobgoblin. It's almost as if he wants me to catch him, you realize. My spider-sense is still buzzing, I can't let down my guard.

On your next swing you shoot a thick rope of webbing right at the Hobgoblin. He tries to dodge, but he's too slow.

"No!" he cries. "I can't let Spider-Man defeat me again! I won't! I won't!"

You flip forward and land right in front of him as he screams in rage, his hands bound.

"Still have to be careful," you say to yourself as you step in quickly. "Say goodnight, Hobby old pal," you quip. With a smashing uppercut, you knock him flat on his back. In a flash you have him tied up tightly.

You straighten up and for the first time you clearly hear the shouts and screams coming from behind you. Turning, you see actors, members of the film crew and policemen come running toward you.

"Stop!" they shout. "Let him go!"

You gaze around and it's as if a mist is lifting from your eyes. With a sinking feeling you realize that somehow you've been tricked. That figure tightly wrapped in your webbing isn't the Hobgoblin at all—it's Chip Alvarez, the director.

Totally embarrassed, you struggle to get him free of the webbing as fast as you can. It doesn't help that he's yelling at you the whole time, and your spider-sense is still buzzing in your head.

"What is the meaning of this?" Alvarez demands. "I'm going to have you arrested!"

There's one person you know who can fool you so completely, and that's Mysterio. But how can you explain that to Alvarez?

"Officer," Alvarez is speaking to one of the policemen who has just arrived. "Arrest Spider-Man. Not only did he attack me, but he let the Hobgoblin go!"

"Hey," you say, trying to defend yourself. "I know this looks bad, but there's a good explanation. And I'll be back with it as soon as I can."

Trying to avoid Alvarez's withering glare, you shoot a web-line at the closest lamppost and swing yourself away from the gathering crowd. Now you figure your best chance at clearing things up is to catch the real Hobgoblin.

He can't have gotten too far, you think while web-slinging yourself to the top of the nearest apartment building. And sure enough, there he is—flying away on his glider.

But as fast as you follow, swinging from building to building, he manages to stay one step ahead of you. He turns west, heading for the Hudson River, and you follow.

Just before the river, the Hobgoblin's jet-glider swoops down and disappears in a tunnel under the West Side Highway. You swing down to street level and run to the tunnel entrance. As cars zoom by overhead, you ponder your options: Should you follow the Hobgoblin into the dark tunnel? Maybe it's a trap and you should wait for him at the other end.

IF YOU FOLLOW THE HOBGOBLIN INTO
THE TUNNEL,
GO TO PAGE 138.

IF YOU DON'T, GO TO PAGE 26.

"*Say goodnight, Gobby old pal,*" *you quip. With a smashing uppercut you knock him flat on his back.*

"I hate to do it, but I have to try to save that creep," you say to Mary Jane. You make her promise to get far away from the rally and the Vulture and then you duck into an alley to change into Spider-Man. The Vulture has picked Mason up and is now flapping around over the crowd, threatening to drop him.

"Stop him, please!" Mason begs you.

If you attack the Vulture he'll probably drop Mason and you might not be able to catch him in time. But if you leave him alone, the Vulture just might kill him. What should you do?

IF YOU ATTACK THE VULTURE,
GO TO PAGE 66.

IF YOU DECIDE TO WAIT,
GO TO PAGE 54.

"I can't chase every police siren I hear," you tell yourself after an agonizing few seconds.

Your spider-sense is still buzzing and that makes you feel weird. Usually it warns you about some immediate danger.

You try to clear your head as you watch Al Markham, the special-effects man, talking to one of his assistants. Curious, you walk over to see what they're doing.

"Hi, I'm Peter Parker," you say, introducing yourself. "I'm Mary Jane's husband."

You stick out your hand and Markham takes it, squeezing it in an iron tight grip.

"Hi," Markham grins.

"Can't talk now," Markham says when you ask what they're doing. "Big scene. But Jerry will show you."

Markham walks away and Jerry, his assistant, holds out his hand. In his palm are some small paper tubes that look like firecrackers. Each one is attached to a wire.

"These are squibs," Jerry explains. "They're small explosives—not very powerful. We use them when we want to make it look like someone's been shot. We put them under the actor's clothing and then set them off with radio controls. The actor wears a pad underneath to protect his skin."

He shows you the radio-control device, a small orange and blue box with a large red button on it.

"All I have to do is push this button and *pow, pow pow!*" says Jerry.

Suddenly your spider-sense kicks in to high gear. Fully alert, you look around you. MJ's stunt double is ready for her scene. Alvarez and the stunt director stand behind the camera. Someone yells, "Action!"

The stuntwoman swings out onto the wire. She's holding on with both hands as she slides out into the air, dangling hundreds of feet above the street. She moves across toward the distant Trump Tower building, pulling herself hand over hand. She's almost there when, suddenly, she stops.

"Hey!" she shouts. "I'm stuck!"

Without waiting another second, you head for the doorway, ducking into the building. Seconds later, you've found an empty office and, in a flash, you've got your uniform and web-shooters on.

"Never fear, Spider-Man is here," you announce grandly. Unfortunately, no one seems to appreciate your dramatics. They're all too busy looking at the stuntwoman, dangling like a doll at the far end of the wire. In the few seconds it took you to change, she's lost her hold and the only thing between her and a deadly drop is her safety line.

"Spider-Man!" shouts Chip Alvarez. "Help her, please!"

Without another thought, you shoot a web-line toward the Trump Tower, kick off from the wall and begin to rush through the air toward the trapped stuntwoman. In a split second you're flying through an arc toward the other building. You're getting ready to shoot another web and change directions to bring you up under the dangling stunt-woman. But as you do, your spider-sense goes crazy again.

What is it? You have only a moment to react. Is your spider-sense telling you *not* to head for the stuntwoman? Or is it telling you she's about to drop to her death? You have to decide—now!

IF YOU GO TOWARD THE
STUNTWOMAN, GO TO PAGE 102.

IF YOU CHANGE YOUR DIRECTION,
GO TO PAGE 9.

Better safe than sorry, you think. It could be my spider-sense is picking up some danger to them, if it's nearby. No one notices as you slip away into the building. In just a few seconds, you've found an empty office, changed into your Spider-Man gear and pushed open a window.

Like a supercharged trapeze artist, you fly from one building to another, shooting new web-lines as you go. You can still hear the police sirens, so you have no trouble following the cars. Just a dozen blocks south you see a whole fleet of police vehicles lined up along one side of the street. A huge crowd on their lunch breaks fills every corner.

You drop down lightly in front of a police captain who seems to be in charge.

"Spider-Man!" he cries with relief. Behind him you can hear the crowd cheering at your arrival. It makes you feel good to know you're appreciated.

"Your friendly *neighborhood* Spider-Man," you correct him. "Can I help, officer?"

"I'll say you can," the cop says. "The Shocker is holed up in that bank over there. He's taken at least twenty people hostage. He says unless we let him go in five minutes, with the money, he's going to start killing them one by one. We're afraid to rush him because some of the hostages might get hurt. Do you think you can get them out of there safely?"

"I'll do my best," you say confidently. You've fought the Shocker many times. He's not usually a match for you, but you're concerned that his vibro-waves—compressed air blasts—can do a lot of damage. He'll be hard to control unless you can wrap him up quickly.

A hostage situation is tricky, you realize as you examine the bank building. If I confront the Shocker directly, innocent people might get hurt. But if I try to sneak them out, I might run out of time before his deadline.

Okay, big hero, you think, which will it be—in the front door or sneak attack?

IF YOU DECIDE TO ATTACK THE SHOCKER DIRECTLY, GO TO PAGE 16.

IF YOU DECIDE TO SNEAK IN THE BUILDING, GO TO PAGE 64.

You sleep fitfully in the hours that are left of the night. In spite of your exhaustion, you're up with the first light of day. MJ is sleeping peacefully beside you, blissfully unaware of all that has happened.

You move about the dark apartment, wondering what to do. When you came in last night, MJ told you that filming on her movie, *Fatal Action III*, is set to resume that morning. Is MJ in danger? And there's a lot more for you to worry about. Like mayoral candidate Bob Mason, or any of those bad guys you've been tangling with over the last few days.

"Morning, Tiger," Mary Jane looks at you sleepily from the bed.

"Up early, aren't you?"

"Yeah," you say, trying to hide your anxiety behind a smile. "I, uh, wanted to make you breakfast."

"Wow!" MJ says with mock surprise. "My web-slinging hubby is going to cook? Do you need help pouring the cereal?"

"Very funny," you laugh, feeling some of the weight lift off your shoulders. "How about some spider-scrambled eggs?"

You walk into the kitchen, get down a frying pan and begin to whip up some eggs. You switch on the radio, just in time to catch the tail end of a news broadcast.

"To repeat, the criminal mastermind known as Doctor Octopus has delivered a threat in the form of a videotaped warning, which was discovered at City Hall just minutes ago. He claims that, assisted by criminals known as the Sinister Six, which includes the Shocker, the Vulture and Spider-Man, he intends to seize and hold a section of Manhattan for ransom. For more on this . . ."

The radio drones on, but you're too angry to hear it.

How can they just swallow that? you ask yourself. They know Spider-Man doesn't work with Doc Ock and those creeps. How can my reputation mean so little?

"Is that coffee I smell?" MJ says, walking in.

"Uh, yeah," you answer, your mind racing. What should you do now? Stay with MJ to protect her, or go out and find the Sinister Six before they do any more damage?

IF YOU STAY WITH MJ,
GO TO PAGE 46.

IF YOU GO IN SEARCH OF THE SINISTER
SIX, GO TO PAGE 94.

I can take the Hobgoblin any day, you think, feeling very sure of yourself as you swing into the darkened tunnel. And I don't want him getting away this time.

Unfortunately, when your spider-sense goes off like a five-alarm fire, it's a split second too late for you to react. In the dark, cramped tunnel, there's not enough room for you to swing around and you plow right into the trap the Hobgoblin has set for you. You collide with shattering force into an open steel cage sitting on the tunnel floor. Your reflexes have you on your feet and twisting about in a flash, but the door of the trap has already snapped shut.

I can take the Hobgoblin easy, but he doesn't always work alone, you remind yourself ruefully.

As if in reaction to your thoughts, six shadowy figures emerge from the gloom of the dank, dark hole. You don't need a light to tell you who they are. It's the Sinister Six: the Vulture, the Hobgoblin, the Shocker, Myst-

As if in reaction to your thoughts, six shadowy figures emerge from the gloom of the dank, dark hole.

erio, the Chameleon and last of all, their demented leader, Doctor Octopus.

"Hey, Ock!" you say, trying to sound glib and confident. "You might as well surrender now. I've got you surrounded."

Doctor Octopus walks right to the cage bars, his weird, metallic arms snaking through the gloom like a nest of vipers.

"Save your jokes, Spider-Man," he growls. In the dim light his eyes are two dark disks behind his glasses. "Today is *our* day to celebrate. We've planned your defeat for a long time—too long! Frankly, I'm disappointed. I'd hoped to prolong your agony, to humiliate you in front of the whole world before your final destruction."

"You know, Ock," you say, "you really ought to get yourself a hobby. Ever think of knitting? You'd be a natural."

"Silence!" Doc Ock roars, his voice echoing off the low ceiling. "*You* are my hobby, Spider-Man, and destroying you is my life's work. Thank you for making it so easy. I didn't think you'd fall for this simple trap, but since you did, we might as well end it now. Say goodbye, Spider-Man."

You have a sinking feeling that this might really be the end.

END

"Spider-Man!" the Hobgoblin cries.

"That's my name, and smashing pumpkins is my game," you answer quickly. "Hey, speaking of smashing pumpkins, have you heard their new CD?" you ask coolly. "I'll be sure to send you one—in prison."

"Very clever, Spider-Man," the Hobgoblin sneers, flying his glider toward you at full speed. "But the only one who's going anywhere is you—straight to the morgue!"

Two pumpkin bombs appear in his hands, and in the blink of an eye they're flying toward you. But you have no trouble dodging them and they explode harmlessly on the armored side of the tank.

The jet-glider has swerved around and the crazed villain is now rushing back to meet you. The glider dips through the air and two more pumpkin bombs come flying your way.

At least the bus and MJ are safe for the moment, you think as you roll away from the shock of the explosions. But why? Why isn't he using the bus as a shield?

The Hobgoblin's glider has come to a stop just a few feet above the street now, and he stands on it, facing you. He holds his hands in the air above his head and delivers a challenge.

"Forget the hostages. Forget the ransom!" he declares. "There's only one thing I really want, and that's your *death*, Spider-Man! Come and meet me face to face, if you dare!"

With a quick glance you see that the bus with the hostages has come to rest on the roof of the museum. They seem out of danger, so you shoot a web-line to the side of the museum and begin to swing out toward the waiting villain. You're in mid-swing when a nagging doubt comes to mind. Can you be *sure* the actors are all right? What about Mary Jane? Maybe you should make sure they're safe first. What do you do?

IF YOU GO AFTER THE HOBGOBLIN,
GO TO PAGE 126.

IF YOU RESCUE THE ACTORS AND MJ,
GO TO PAGE 22. .

"That's it, Shocker, you win!" you shout as you swing away from the bank. "I'm getting out of here while I can!"

"You can't escape that easily!" the Shocker replies. He runs after you.

You lead the Shocker along, looking for an empty spot where you can fight him safely. Then you see your chance—a large construction site. Rising from the cement are the beginnings of the steel skeleton of a new office tower. You swing from your webbing and drop on top of the fence surrounding the site.

"End of the line," you say to the brown-and-yellow costumed villain.

"Tired of running, Spider-Man?" the Shocker sneers at you.

"Prepare yourself for a shock," you answer. "I was just trying to get you away from those hostages."

"Really?" the Shocker answers. "Well, here's a shock for you. I was just trying to get away with the money—and I did."

143

And before you can stop him, he lifts his arms and sends an air blast at one of the steel girders in the building site. The entire skeleton starts to lean at a crazy angle.

"Help!"

You look up and see three construction workers clinging to the top of the steel structure.

"Hold on, fellas!" you shout and race toward them.

"Go be a hero, Spider-Man," the Shocker taunts you as he runs in the other direction. "And thanks for getting me out of that jam!"

Just as you lower the last worker to safety, the police arrive.

"Where's the Shocker?" the police captain asks.

"He got away," you say sheepishly.

"He just let him *walk* away," says one of the construction workers you rescued.

"Is that true, Spider-Man?" says the captain.

"I had to," you say. You try to explain, but it sounds like you're just making excuses.

GO TO PAGE 31.